Praise for Ally B  ...Song

"This is a story of pain and loss but more importantly it is the story of the ultimate redemptive and healing powers of love."

-- Christina, *Romance Junkies*

"The plotline is very intriguing and kept me on the edge of my seat waiting to see what would happen next. *Forgotten Song* is a keeper!"

-- Susan White, *Coffee Time Romance*

"I had to read it front to back without stopping and I loved it. This is a must read."

-- Teresa, *Fallen Angel Reviews*

"Forgotten Song is a beautifully written tale of a man who is badly damaged by events of his past... I was very touched by Eric and Ben's dedication to each other..."

-- Chrissy, *Euro-Reviews*

Loose Id®

ISBN 10: 1-59632-732-4
ISBN 13: 978-1-59632-732-0
FORGOTTEN SONG
Copyright © June 2008 by Ally Blue
Originally released in e-book format in July 2005

Cover Art and Design by April Martinez

DISCLAIMER: Many of the acts described in our BDSM/fetish titles can be dangerous. Please do not try any new sexual practice, whether it be fire, rope, or whip play, without the guidance of an experienced practitioner. Neither Loose Id nor its authors will be responsible for any loss, harm, injury or death resulting from use of the information contained in any of its titles.

This book is an original publication of Loose Id. Each individual story herein was previously published in e-book format only by Loose Id and is a work of fiction. Any similarity to actual persons, events or existing locations is entirely coincidental.

Printed in the U.S.A. by
Lightning Source, Inc.
1246 Heil Quaker Blvd
La Vergne TN 37086
www.lightningsource.com

FORGOTTEN SONG

Ally Blue

Dedication

Dedication: To the girls (and boys) of the Cheesecake. You know who you are. This book would not have happened without you.

*"To love a person is to learn the song
That is in their heart,
And to sing it to them
When they have forgotten"*

-- Anonymous

Chapter One

The first time I laid eyes on Eric, he was kicking a guy twice his size in the balls. Probably not the smartest move in the world. But that's Eric for you. He's all fire and temper and not much restraint. Not that I knew that at the time.

I had just finished my shift at Marco's, a little Italian place with the best brick-oven pizza in the world, and had decided to walk the few blocks to my favorite bar, The Alley Kat. My band played there every Friday night, and I knew the staff and all the regular customers. This wasn't Friday, but I usually went on over after work if I could. It was dark and noisy and friendly, and I liked hanging out there.

I strolled down the street past closed shops and open bars, whistling a Beck tune and thinking about nothing much. The night was cool and smelled like coffee and Thai food, like most summer nights in Asheville. It's not a big city, but it's got enough personality and atmosphere for ten cities. Just the sort of place where you'd expect exciting things to happen. Still, you never think those exciting things are going to happen to you, do you? They always happen to someone else.

Not this time.

When I rounded the corner onto Lexington, where The Alley Kat was located, I nearly ran smack into two guys fighting. One was huge, at least six-foot-seven and wide as a door. You'd have thought he'd be the one winning, since the other one was easily a foot shorter and a hundred pounds lighter. My size, more or less. But no, the big guy was bent double with the little guy's foot buried in his groin.

"Fucking brainless asshole!" the smaller man shouted. "Don't you fucking touch me again! I'll rip your goddamn arms off and shove 'em up your ass!"

I stopped and stared at him. His fists were clenched so hard his knuckles were white, and he was shaking. The guy he'd kicked was still doubled over, cursing under his breath. I didn't know either of them, but it looked to me like somebody was about to get seriously hurt. Before I could wade right into the middle of it, the bar door opened and Malcolm stepped out.

Malcolm's a bartender at the Alley Kat. The place doesn't have a regular bouncer. Normally, they don't need one. But if that sort of situation ever comes up, Malcolm handles it. He's not a particularly big guy, but he's calm and clear-headed and can usually stop a fight before it starts. He walked up to the two other men. I hung back out of the way and took my cell phone out just in case.

"Break it up, guys," Malcolm said.

"Fuck you!" the little guy shouted. "This is between me and him!"

Malcolm shook his head. "Not here, man. If you're gonna fight, take it someplace else." He turned to the big man, who was now standing more or less straight. "You need to see a doctor?"

The man shook his head. "I'm fine. He's a fucking psycho though." He pointed an extremely large finger at the guy who'd kicked him. "You should be more careful, boy. You never know who you're pissing off."

He turned and hobbled down the sidewalk. Malcolm stared after him with a frown.

I saw the punch coming, but didn't have time to warn Malcolm. Before I could make a sound, the stranger had landed a hard right to Malcolm's jaw and Malcolm went down.

Now normally, I'm not a fighter. I can take care of myself, but most other guys are just bigger than me. Fact of life. It usually keeps me from starting something I can't finish. Seeing that guy hit Malcolm when he wasn't looking, though, pissed me off. I strode up to him.

"Hey, what the fuck's your problem?" I managed not to shout.

He turned and pinned me with the most intense stare I'd ever seen. His eyes, deep blue and sparking with fury, stopped me cold.

"Fuck off!" he spat.

I felt my face flush. "Look, dickhead, Malcolm's my friend, and you are not. Leave him alone."

He smiled in a way I didn't like one bit. "Oh, you want some too? Bring it on, man, bring it on."

I didn't much want to bring it on. He was small, but he was built like a panther: all lean muscle and coiled energy. He looked like he knew how to hurt a person, and I wasn't sure I could hold my own against him. He started toward me with murder in his eyes and I braced myself for a fight. It didn't happen. Malcolm was back on his feet by then, and he grabbed the guy's arm before he could get any closer.

To this day, I've never seen a look of such pure terror on a person's face. He stopped dead in his tracks and his eyes went wide and blank. Then before I knew what was happening, he twisted free, whirled around and kicked Malcolm in the knee. Malcolm went down again, clutching his leg and cussing a blue streak.

That was it for me. I closed the distance between us, grabbed the stranger's wrist before he could turn around and twisted his arm up behind his back.

I expected him to struggle, or kick or something, but he didn't. He went perfectly still in my grip. It confused me, to say the least. He said something I couldn't quite catch and I leaned closer.

"Let me go, just, just let me go now, please..." His voice was barely louder than a whisper and I could feel him shaking. I frowned.

"How do I know you won't sucker punch me?"

He half-turned his face to me and I frowned harder. He was white as paper, his eyes were panicky, and he was breathing way too fast.

"I-I won't, please let me go now, okay? Don't, don't hurt him…me, don't hurt me."

I was totally lost by that time. He wasn't making any sense. But it was pretty obvious that he was close to losing it completely. Malcolm had pushed himself upright again and leaned against the wall of the bar, safely out of reach. So I let go of the guy's arm and stepped back. He turned toward me, licked his lips, and opened his mouth like he was going to say something. Before he could speak, his eyes rolled back and he dropped to the ground.

"Aw, shit!" I knelt beside him and rolled him gently onto his back.

"What the hell just happened?" Malcolm hopped over to us.

"Not a clue. I didn't hurt him, man, you saw."

Malcolm studied him for a minute. "I think maybe we ought to call 911. He's bleeding."

He sure was. He'd hit his head on the sidewalk when he fell and blood was seeping from what was sure to be one spectacular goose-egg later on. I nodded and flipped open my cell phone.

The guy's eyes popped opened and he watched with a frown as I started to dial. Something seemed to click in his brain suddenly and he grabbed the phone out of my hand.

"Hey!" I protested. "What the hell are you doing?"

"Don't call the cops. I'm leaving now, okay? Sorry, I'm sorry I hit you, man, you just scared me is all. I don't like to be touched."

Shaking my head, I plucked my cell back out of his hand. "It was him you hit, not me. And I'm not calling the cops, I'm calling an ambulance. You need to go to the emergency room."

If I thought he'd be relieved by that, I was sorely disappointed. He sucked in a sharp breath and sat straight up. His eyes went unfocused for a second and he laid a hand over the big purple bruise already forming on one side of his forehead.

"No," he said. "I can't go to the hospital."

"Look, you passed out cold for no good reason, and you hit your head." Impatiently I gestured to the bleeding lump on his forehead. "You could be hurt worse than you think."

He shook his head carefully. "I'm fine. Just haven't eaten in a while is all, that's probably why I passed out. I appreciate the concern, but I'm fine, really. I've gotta go now."

He levered himself to his feet and stood there swaying. Malcolm and I glanced at each other. I knew we were both thinking the same thing: this guy needed a doctor, but how could we make him go? We couldn't, of course. So we stood and watched as he started to make his way down the sidewalk.

He didn't get far. He managed a few shaky steps, then fell to his hands and knees and threw up. Or maybe I should say dry-heaved, since nothing came up at all. I went over and crouched down beside him.

"You ready to go to the ER now?"

He shook his head. "Not going."

"Why the hell not?"

"I-I don't have any insurance. I can't pay."

"Doesn't matter, man, they'll treat you anyway. You might have to pay them back five dollars at a time for the rest of your life, but they'll treat you."

He turned to look at me, and it suddenly struck me how good looking he was underneath the dirt and bruises. Light brown hair stuck up in all directions, like he'd blindfolded himself and cut it with garden shears. His skin was smooth and seemed to be naturally pale even when it wasn't dead white like it was now. His mouth was full and soft and turned up just a little at the corners, giving his face a certain sweetness behind the fear and anger.

His lips moved and I realized he was saying something. I shook myself. "What?"

"I said, I'm not going. I just...I don't like hospitals, that's all."

My resolve began to weaken. I've always been a sucker for a pair of big blue eyes, and damn if his weren't the prettiest I'd seen in a long time. I sighed and clicked the phone closed. He visibly sagged with relief.

"Where do you live?" Malcolm asked. "I'll call you a taxi."

He sat back and stared hard at the ground. "I just got into town. I don't exactly have any place yet. It's okay, really. I already feel better. I can walk down to the shelter. I know where it is."

He pushed to his feet again. I stood too, watching him. He still didn't look so good to me. When his knees buckled, I caught him and lowered him gently to the ground. He pushed me away and scooted out of reach.

"You can't even stand up." I looked him up and down. He was dirty, his clothes were stained and the dark smudges under his eyes told me he hadn't slept in a long time. "You said you hadn't eaten in a while; how long's it been exactly? And when's the last time you got any sleep?"

He gave me a wry smile. "'Bout three days, I guess."

I nodded. "That does it. You're coming home with me."

Chapter Two

To say that he was not happy with that plan would be an understatement. He shook his head in protest and stared at me like a rabbit watching a pack of dogs.

"Oh, no, no, no, I'm not going anywhere with you. No."

"Hey, man, come on, you know you're in no shape to be out on the streets right now. I'm a nice guy, really, you can trust me." I reached a hand toward him and he recoiled as if I'd hit him. His eyes met mine, and his fear was plain to see.

"I can't trust anybody." I didn't know what to say to that.

He started to stand, fell to his knees again, and shoved me away when I went to help him up. He tried again, got to his feet by sheer willpower, and staggered over to lean against the wall. He stood there gasping for breath. His heart was pounding so hard I could see the pulse jumping in his throat.

I stepped over to Malcolm's side, keeping a watchful eye on the stranger. "Hey, Malcolm, are Mike and Janey in there?"

He nodded. "Yeah, been here about an hour or so."

"Could you tell them to come out here? I need Mike to drive us."

Malcolm grinned at me. "'Us', huh? Don't you think you're being a little overly optimistic? He's not gonna go anywhere without a fight."

I shrugged. "I think I can convince him."

He laughed. "You just want to take him home 'cause he's so pretty."

"No, I don't." I could feel myself blushing and knew he was at least partly right. Yeah, I'm gay. And I had to admit that I was attracted to this guy. I do like to think, though, that I've never taken advantage of someone's pain and suffering just to get into their pants.

I glanced over at the subject of our discussion. He still leaned heavily on the wall, staring into space. I clapped Malcolm on the shoulder as he limped inside and then cautiously approached the stranger. He didn't seem to notice me. He jumped when I cleared my throat, but his eyes focused on my face again.

"What's your name?"

He stared at me for a long time before answering. "Eric."

"Well, Eric, you have a choice to make. My place, or the hospital. Now which is it gonna be?"

Something dangerous slid through his eyes, and I stepped back a pace out of pure instinct.

"Neither." His voice was low and controlled, but panic boiled just under the surface. "Just leave me the fuck alone."

I shook my head, and wondered exactly how stupid I was being. "Look, you need someone to look out for you, and you can't get that at the shelter. There's too damn many people staying there, and not nearly enough staff to keep up. I'm not taking you there, and I think you know you can't walk that far. So?"

He glared at me and I glared back. I didn't back down because I was right, and we both knew it. Finally he looked away.

"Okay, fine, I guess I'll go to your place."

"Good. I'm Ben, by the way, Ben Carson. Nice to meet you."

He stared at me like I'd just sprouted a second head and I blushed. I mentally cursed the Irish genes that gave me my fair skin and blond curls. Usually, I didn't blush this damn easy, but when I did, it showed. I met his gaze and gave him a tentative smile. He smiled back at me, and I forgot to breathe for a second. His smile lit up his whole face and suddenly he was beautiful.

"You're a strange one, Ben. I usually scare people off."

I had to swallow twice before I could talk again. "Yeah, well, I don't scare easy."

"I can see that." His eyes held mine and I couldn't look away. Not that I wanted to. "You seem like a nice guy."

"I am."

"I'm not."

"I don't believe you. Everybody's got some good in them."

For a split second his guard dropped and a bottomless pit of sorrow opened in his eyes. It shook me to the core. Then the walls went back up and it was gone.

"Not everyone." The emptiness in his voice chilled me.

I wanted to ask what he meant, and what the hell had happened to him to make him like this. But I didn't. He probably wouldn't answer me anyway. We were still staring at each other when I heard the door open behind me, followed by Mike and Janey's voices.

Janey Hanson's my best friend. We've known each other since high school, and we've always been close. We met Mike Donelly at a youth hostel in Germany the summer after our college graduation He was spending the summer traveling through Europe, same as us. Mike and Janey fell head over heels for each other, and when we got back to the States he left his home town of Denver and moved in with Janey. Didn't even think twice about it. That was three years ago, and they've been joined at the hip ever since.

"Ben!" Mike called as he and Janey walked over. "What's up, man?" His dark eyes flicked curiously in Eric's direction but he didn't say anything.

"Guys, this is Eric, he's gonna be staying with me for a while. Eric, this is Mike and Janey. We need a ride home, Mike, can you drive us?"

"Sure. Hang on; I'll go get the car. Good to meet you, Eric." Mike strolled off down the street without waiting for an answer.

Janey turned wide gray eyes to me and frowned, and I knew what was coming. I was always picking up strays, and Janey was always nagging me about how dangerous it was to take in some stranger off the street. Grabbing her hand, I silently begged her to just this once not say anything. She gave me a look that said I was in for a lecture later and turned to Eric with a sweet smile.

"So, Eric. Where are you from?"

He narrowed his eyes at her. "City in southern Alabama. Mobile."

She crossed her arms and pursed her lips. "Hm. So. Eric, huh? Eric what?"

"Eric none-of-your-fucking-business, that's what."

She shook her head. "Oh, yeah, Ben, you sure can pick 'em," she muttered as she turned and walked away.

Mike pulled up to the curb, reached behind him and opened the door to the back seat. I turned to Eric and held out my hand. He just stared at me.

"Come on, I'm just gonna help you to the car. Your knees are shaking."

Eric stared hard at me for a few seconds, then finally took my hand. I'd be lying if I said it didn't feel good, in spite of the circumstances. He took a step forward, swayed and nearly fell again, and I wrapped an arm around his waist before he could protest. He gasped out loud and tried to pull away, but I wouldn't let him.

"I'm not gonna hurt you, Eric," I whispered. "Relax."

He gave me a look that clearly said he wasn't so sure. But he let me help him into the car. I think he knew damn well that he was too weak and shaky to manage alone.

We rode back to our apartment building in silence. It was a short trip. Janey, Mike, and I only live a few minutes from downtown where the Alley Kat is, but it seemed like it took hours. I kept trying to look at Eric without seeming to.

Something about him tugged at my mind and made me want to know more. And it wasn't just his gorgeous blue eyes, or his kissable mouth, or the way his jeans molded his body. He just had a spark in him that called to me. I can't explain it any better than that.

"Okay, boys and girls," Mike called out as he parked and killed the motor. "Home sweet home."

I opened the door and stepped out and held my hand out for Eric. He took a deep breath and I could tell he was still a little unsure, but he took my hand. With my arm around his waist to steady him, we made our slow way inside. Janey took my keys and ran ahead to open the door. Inside I lowered Eric carefully to the bed, thankful yet again for my first floor apartment. Eric curled up on his side without a word.

"Ben," Janey said, "could I talk to you for a minute?"

Uh-oh, I thought, here it comes. I glanced at Mike in desperation. He shrugged and gave me a sympathetic smile, but didn't say anything. I sighed and followed Janey out into the hall. Mike hurried across the hall and into their apartment.

"Thanks for nothing, dude," I muttered under my breath as he slammed the door. Squaring my shoulders, I turned and faced Janey.

"Ben, what the hell do you think you're doing?" She crossed her arms and frowned fiercely at me. It wouldn't have been particularly intimidating to most people, Janey being five-foot-nothing and delicate as a porcelain doll, but I knew her. Looks can be deceiving.

"Lay off, Janey. He hasn't slept or eaten in three days, and he doesn't have any place to go. I didn't want him to have to stay at the shelter in his condition."

She raised her eyebrows at me. "Oh really? And what condition is that? And how does that translate into you having to take care of him?"

"He got in a fight with some guy. Long story short, Malcolm and I both sort of got involved. But before it could get too ugly Eric passed out cold and banged his head on the sidewalk. He was so shaky and sick after that, it sort of scared me to think of him being at the shelter, you know? And he wouldn't let me take him to the ER. Said he didn't like hospitals."

Janey nodded and twirled a strand of blond and blue striped hair around her finger. "So you thought you'd just bring him home, huh?"

"Well, yeah. He needs someone to look after him."

"That's what you always say. News flash, Ben, you can't save the whole world. Sometimes you just need to leave it alone."

I shook my head. "You know I can't do that."

She sighed. "Yeah. You're the most generous person I know, and I really wouldn't change that. I just hope you never have reason to regret it."

She stood up on tiptoe and kissed my cheek, then turned and went into her apartment. I shook my head and opened the door to my own place.

A full-time waiter and part-time musician can't afford much of an apartment, and this one sure as hell wasn't much.

The door opened directly into a small L-shaped kitchen. A short hallway to the left led to a combination living room and bedroom, with a tiny bathroom tucked into the corner. Barely room to turn around, but it was clean and cheap and had great big windows that let in the sun year round. I liked it just fine.

Eric lay curled on the bed where I'd left him. He seemed to be asleep. I approached as quietly as I could, knelt on the floor beside the bed, and just looked at him. He seemed so small and fragile in sleep, it was hard to believe this was the same guy who'd taken down two men bigger than him just a little while ago. Looking over his body, I noticed for the first time that he was barefoot. His feet were black with grime and covered in cuts and scrapes. He needed a bath pretty bad, but I hated to wake him for that.

I looked back up at his face. The cut on his head had nearly stopped bleeding. The edges of the wound were covered in a crust of dried blood, but the center still glistened red. I reached out and brushed a finger over the huge bruise blossoming under the blood and dirt. Suddenly, a hand clamped down hard on my wrist and I jumped. Eric's eyes were wide open and staring into mine.

"Jesus, you scared me. I thought you were asleep."

He smiled grimly. "I sleep light. What're you doing?"

"Nothing, just looking at this cut on your head. You ought to let me clean that before you go to sleep again. It might get infected."

He stared up at me with a puzzled frown. "Why are you being so nice to me?"

"Because you need that right now. Everybody needs help now and then."

"You don't know anything about me."

I shrugged. "Does it matter? I still want to help you."

"Even after what I did to your friend?"

"That pissed me off," I conceded, "but I get the feeling there's more to it than meets the eye. I can let it slide, as long as it doesn't get to be a habit."

He shook his head. "I don't understand you at all."

"Nothing to understand. I always try to help out when I can."

I smiled at him and his face softened. "Thanks, man. Really."

"No problem." I stood and went into the bathroom, and came back out with a wet washcloth. He eyed it suspiciously.

"Just gonna clean off that cut on your head, okay?"

He didn't try to stop me when I knelt down again and pressed the cloth gently to the raw wound. He kept perfectly still and silent while I washed the dirt and blood off. After I'd rinsed out the washcloth twice, the wound finally looked clean. It was still pulsing blood though, so I fished around in my bathroom cabinet until I found some gauze pads and medical tape, and put a bandage on it.

Eric reached up and touched the gauze gingerly. "That's gonna be ugly tomorrow."

"It's already ugly."

He laughed. "Yeah, I guess it probably is."

I grinned at him, then went back into the bathroom, grabbed a clean cloth and towel, filled a plastic basin with warm water, and brought the whole business back into the bedroom. Eric gazed at me with apprehension in his eyes as I set the bucket on the floor and spread out the towel.

"What are you doing now?"

I glanced up at him and had a feeling he wasn't going to like this much. "I'm gonna wash your feet."

"What?" He sat up, went deathly pale and had to lean forward to keep from passing out again. "Why?"

I sighed. This, I thought, is getting old. "They're filthy. I'm cleaning them before you go to bed, that's all."

He opened his mouth to argue, saw the determined look in my eyes, and closed it again. He nodded silently.

"Finally, a little cooperation," I teased. He glared at me but didn't say anything.

I reached out to roll up the bottoms of his jeans. He let me, but he obviously wasn't very happy about it. When I guided his feet into the warm water, he let out a sigh of pleasure.

"Damn, that does feel good." He leaned back on his hands and wiggled his toes.

"Those are gonna have to soak for a little while. You want something to eat?"

He grimaced. "Not right now. Been too long, I think it'd just make me sick."

"How about a soda?"

"Oh, man, that would be great, thanks!"

I got up and went to get a can of cola out of the fridge. He drank half of it in one gulp.

"Fuck, that's the best thing I ever tasted," he gasped when he finally had to come up for air. He smiled at me and my stomach did flip-flops. Damn, he was hot. "Thanks, Ben. I mean it. I know I can be a pain in the ass, but I really do appreciate your taking care of me like this. I'll find a way to pay you back once I get on my feet again."

I shook my head. "Don't worry about it."

His gaze flicked down my body and I felt a surge of desire go through me. I couldn't keep what I was feeling out of my eyes, so I looked at the floor instead.

"Okay, well, uh, I think, I think you've soaked enough, I'm gonna wash 'em now." My voice sounded shaky and breathless and I hated it. If he noticed, he didn't let on.

Kneeling, I lifted one foot out of the water, picked up the washcloth, and started scrubbing the dirt away. He didn't make a sound, but judging by the tension in his leg, it made him uncomfortable. I tried to think of some way to distract him, and finally decided to just give in to my natural curiosity and see what I could find out about him.

"You said you were from Alabama, right?" He nodded. "So how'd you end up in North Carolina?"

He shrugged. "I needed to get away. Heard Asheville was the place to go if you're gay."

I glanced up at him. "You're gay?"

"Yeah, is that a problem?"

His voice was calm, but I could hear the defensiveness. I understood that. Hell, I'd had my back against the wall a few times myself, and I was born and raised here. Asheville's a haven for gays, but sometimes the bastards get to you, even here.

"Nope, I'm gay too. And you heard right, this is the place to be."

His face broke into a smile so beautiful that I had to stop myself from jumping up and shoving my tongue down his throat. It was the most relaxed I'd seen him look, and for a second I wondered if his whole problem was simply fear of gay-bashing. Then I remembered the terror in his eyes when Malcolm had grabbed his arm. His near panic at any unwanted contact, and I knew there had to be more to it than that. Someone, somewhere had damaged him badly. I wanted to know who, and how, and why. And I wanted to take the fear out of his eyes for good.

"Ben?" His voice was wary again, and I realized I'd stopped washing his foot and was simply sitting there on my knees staring at him hard enough to burn holes in him. I shook myself.

"Sorry, just zoned out there for a second. I don't mean to be nosy, but how the hell did you end up barefoot? Your feet are pretty cut up."

They were, too. Small cuts and bruises in various stages of healing covered both feet and ankles, and the soles were ragged.

"I had to leave town in kind of a hurry. Didn't have time to do anything but run out the door."

Now I was dying to know what the hell that was all about. But I figured I'd pushed him enough for one night. He wasn't likely to tell me anything else just yet, and if I kept bugging him, he'd never trust me. And I realized with a shock that I wanted him to.

A few minutes later his feet were clean and glowed pink from the scrubbing. After drying them off with the towel, I stood and stretched.

"Okay, all done." I grinned at him. "You're a good patient."

"And you're a good nurse." He laughed. "I feel a thousand times better now. Thanks."

"My pleasure." It was true, even his feet were sexy.

Something went through his eyes. A heavy sort of look. My pulse sped up and I could feel myself getting hard. I bit my lip and fought it. Suddenly he let out a huge yawn and the moment passed.

"You must be beat. Go on and get some sleep. You can take the bed; I'll sleep on the floor."

He looked horrified. "I can't do that."

"Yeah, you can." I grabbed a pillow off the bed and a blanket off the shelf. "And you will. Get out of those dirty clothes, too; you can borrow something of mine if you want."

"Naw, it's okay."

He pulled his T-shirt over his head and tossed it on the floor, then stood on shaky legs and slid out of his jeans. I stared like an idiot. His body was lean and slender and drop dead gorgeous in nothing but a pair of black boxer-briefs. By the time my lust-addled brain noticed the scars, he'd slipped under the covers and his eyes were drifting closed.

"Thanks, Ben," he murmured drowsily. "'Night."

"'Night." I turned off the light, stripped off my clothes and pulled on a pair of cutoff sweatpants. By the time I finished brushing my teeth, Eric was fast asleep.

I walked over and stood looking down at him. Light from the street lamps outside bathed his face in a soft white glow. His full lips were parted just a little and his long lashes cast feathery shadows on his cheeks. He had a quiet, otherworldly sort of beauty, the sort that gets under your skin before you notice what's happening. My insides did a funny little twist. I'd only known him for an hour or so, but I already wanted to hold him in my arms and protect him from the world.

I traced a finger down his cheek. His skin was smooth and silky, softer than anything I'd ever felt. His mouth looked so sweet and ripe. The urge to bend down and kiss those lips was nearly irresistible. I tiptoed into the bathroom and jerked off, thinking of his luscious mouth and soft pale skin. Then I settled on the floor and lay awake into the small hours.

Chapter Three

The sun was in my eyes when I woke the next morning. I pulled the pillow over my head and tried to remember why the hell I was on the floor. Then heard the toilet flush and everything came back. I sat up just as the bathroom door opened.

"Hi," I said as Eric shuffled back to the bed and plopped down. "How are you feeling?"

He shrugged. "Okay, I guess. Little bit of a headache, but it's not too bad. I look like I got hit by a train though."

I grinned. He did look banged up. A big, ugly black and purple bruise spread from under the bandage on the left side of his forehead to cover part of his cheek, and his eye was swollen. The blood on the bandage had dried to a deep reddish brown.

"That is a nasty bruise, but at least the cut's stopped bleeding."

He nodded. "Yeah. Hey, Ben, would it be okay if I use your shower?"

"Sure, there's clean towels in there on the shelf."

"Thanks." He stood and stretched and my brain promptly stopped working. Jesus, his body was perfect.

Okay, nearly perfect.

I got a better look at the scars this time, and my mouth went dry. A long, thin pink line, obviously from some kind of surgery, started just under his ribs and ran down the middle of his abdomen until it disappeared under the edge of his underwear. Several small round scars dotted his belly, and one larger than the rest puckered the skin on one side of his ribcage. But the one that caught the eye cut a long, wide, jagged path halfway across his stomach. I couldn't even imagine what could've made a scar like that, or the amount of pain that must've gone with it.

"Did you get a good enough look?"

Eric's voice dripped with anger, and I realized I was staring. "Shit, I'm sorry."

"Yeah, well. Not too pretty, are they?"

I looked up at his face and caught a glimpse of a hurt so deep that it made me ache to see it. Then the tough-guy mask was back in place and the pain was gone like it had never been there. I knew what I'd seen, though, and I swore to myself right then to help him heal whatever wounds he still had.

"What happened?" I didn't really expect an answer, but I had to ask. He sat staring at the floor for a while, twisting his fingers together.

"Got jumped by five guys." He looked down at his chest. "The big scar there is where one of them cut me open with a butcher knife. Most of the rest are from surgeries and stuff. I was in the hospital for six weeks. That was nine months ago."

He broke off and rubbed both hands over his face, as if he was trying to scrub away the memory. Sitting back down on the bed, he leaned his elbows on his knees and rested his head in his palms. He looked so lost right then, that all I wanted to do was comfort him. I stood up and went over to sit down beside him. He didn't move. I touched his shoulder and he jumped, but stayed put.

"That explains a lot. I'm sorry. It must've been awful."

He turned his head and stared at me with hope and suspicion fighting for territory on his face. "Yeah, it was. But I don't want to talk about it."

I nodded. "Sure."

My hand still rested on his shoulder. I wanted to run my palm down his bare back and trace my fingers up his spine. Nothing good could come of that, so I restrained myself. Instead, I moved to touch a starburst of white scar tissue on his collarbone. It looked older than the other scars.

"What's this one from?"

He looked startled, then his face went perfectly blank. "Accident. When I was a kid. I'm gonna shower now, if that's okay?"

"Sure, go ahead." He got up without a word, strode into the bathroom and slammed the door behind him. I heard the click of the lock being turned.

"Fuck, was it something I said?" I muttered to myself.

I sat down in my only chair and thought while the shower ran. Eric had told me a little about himself, sure, but I still didn't know much. Hell, I didn't even know his last name. All I knew for sure was that he was from Alabama,

and that something horrible had happened to him. The
attack he'd survived couldn't be the whole story. There had
to be something else, something that terrified him to the
point that he ran away with nothing but the clothes on his
back.

He was a man with secrets, and I wanted to know what
they were.

"Um, Ben?"

Eric's voice snapped me out of my thoughts. I looked up.
He stood in the doorway in nothing but a towel, with water
trickling down his chest. He looked positively edible. I
clasped my hands together and successfully stifled the urge
to pull the towel off and lick him all over.

"Hey. Feeling better?"

"Yeah. Listen, I'm sorry about how I acted, it's just that
what gave me this scar?" He touched the place on his
collarbone. "It fucked me up for years and it's still hard to
talk about it. And after everything that happened later on... I
get freaked out sometimes. Sorry."

"Hey, man, it's okay. You don't have to tell me what
happened if you don't want, but you know you can, right? I
mean I know we don't really know each other yet, but I'd
like to get to know you better. And I'm a good listener if you
ever need one."

He gave me a smile that made me tingle from head to
toe. "Thanks, Ben. Never thought I'd say this, but I'd kind of
like to get to know you better too." He shook his head and
laughed. "It's funny. I've never felt so comfortable, so fast
with anyone except..."

He stopped suddenly and the color drained from his face. I jumped up, a little alarmed.

"Eric, you okay?" I touched his arm. His eyes focused on me, and if I didn't know better I'd have said he was afraid; not of me this time, but for me. "Eric?"

He nodded and let me help him into the chair. "Yeah, I'm fine. Damn. Sorry. It's just…" He stared at me, chewing on his lip. "Okay, look. I'm planning to stay in Asheville for a long time, maybe forever. And I'd like us to be friends."

"Me too." That wasn't all I wanted, but I wasn't about to say that right then.

He smiled. "Good. But listen, if we're gonna be friends, then you need to know something."

I gulped. "I'm listening."

He took a deep breath. "I told you about those guys attacking me. Well, that's not the only baggage I've got. There's lots more. Lots. I get panic attacks sometimes, or I'll see some sort of connection between the past and the present and it scares me. Like just now."

"What was it?"

"I can't tell you. Not yet. The shrink at the hospital said I had to work on being direct and honest and not hiding from the things that had happened to me, and God knows I'm trying, but it's hard." He laughed. "You have no idea what a huge step it was for me to tell you as much as I have already. Dr. Hendrix would be proud. I only got a few sessions, 'cause I didn't have the money to keep going after I got out of the hospital, but it helped."

He fell silent. I wanted to ask him why he'd left Mobile in such a hurry, but I didn't think he'd answer. And he'd just trusted me with what was, for him, a huge chunk of personal information. I had to respect that, which meant letting him take his time in revealing more.

Changing the subject seemed like a good idea. "Hey, you've gotta be starved this morning, why don't I make us some breakfast? I'm not much of a cook, but I do okay with scrambled eggs and toast."

"Oh yeah, that sounds great! You're right, I am starved."

"I bet. Three days with no food is a long time. How come you didn't eat? I know there's got to be shelters or something where you could've gotten fed on the way up here."

"Well, it wasn't a money thing. I have money. A little bit, anyway. I just didn't want to go. You never know who's gonna be there."

That didn't make any damn sense to me. But he had his poker face on, which I was already learning meant he didn't want to talk. So I put an iron lid on my curiosity and let the subject drop.

"All right, scrambled eggs coming right up. Go on and get dressed while I cook. You can borrow some of my clothes; I think we're about the same size. I don't have to go to work 'til about four, so maybe we could head downtown after a while and buy you some clothes, huh?"

He stirred uncomfortably. "No, that's okay. They've probably got extra clothes at the shelter. I can borrow some of those and get mine washed."

It killed me that he assumed he was going back out on the street. I didn't know if it was because he didn't want to stay with me or if he thought I wanted him gone now that he was feeling better, but he obviously thought the one night was all he got.

"You don't have to leave." He raised his eyebrows at me and I blushed. "You can stay with me as long as you want. It gets old being by myself anyhow; it'll be nice to have someone to talk to."

He stared at me until I started to fidget. "I'd like that," he finally said. "Thanks."

I just grinned at him. He grinned back at me and I headed for the kitchen feeling decidedly giddy.

He was dressed and in the kitchen with me before I'd finished cooking the eggs. I almost let the toast burn because the sight of him in my jeans, barefoot and bare-chested, turned my brains to soup. He raked a hand through his wet hair and I dropped the butter knife on the floor.

"Oops." I bent to pick the knife up and he raised an eyebrow at me.

"Coffee?" he asked.

"Freezer."

"What?"

"Freezer," I repeated. "Keeps it fresher."

"If you say so." He pulled the bag of French roast out of the freezer and started making a pot.

A few minutes later we sat down at my tiny kitchen table to eat. Eric inhaled his whole plateful before I was halfway done with mine, then sat back with a sigh.

"Damn, that sure hit the spot." He grinned. "You cook okay for a single guy."

"Thanks, I think."

"You are single, aren't you?"

I tried to act casual, though my pulse was pounding suddenly. "Last time I checked."

He leaned forward on his elbows and studied my face with an intensity that made me squirm in my seat.

"What?" I demanded.

He smiled. "You make me think of my sister, Sarah."

"Your sister, huh? Maybe I should grow a beard."

"That's not what I meant." He laughed. "You don't look like a girl. Not at all."

He gave me a distinctly appreciative once-over and I nearly swallowed my fork. Eric bit his lip and choked back a laugh.

"Funny. So why do I remind you of your sister?"

He smiled again, and this time it was a sad smile. "It's your eyes. That really dark brown. She loved that color; used to call 'em Tootsie Roll eyes. She swore a person had to be one of the good guys if they had 'em, because anyone with eyes like candy had to be sweet."

I didn't know what to say. The thrill that went through me at his roundabout way of calling me sweet was dampened by the sadness I felt from him. Something in his face told me Sarah wasn't in his life anymore, and I wasn't sure how to acknowledge that without making him shut down again. But he brought it up, so maybe he wanted to talk.

"What happened to her?"

He stared down at the table. "She died fifteen years ago. I was ten."

"Oh, man, I'm sorry." I reached out and took his hand. He looked startled for a second, then his fingers curled around mine and I wished I could stop time. "You must miss her a lot, huh?"

A strange look passed over his face and was gone before I could figure it out. He nodded. "Yeah. She had a rough life, and we weren't all that close toward the end. But I remember her when she was...well, before those last months, and I do miss her."

He raised his eyes to mine, and I could feel how much he wanted to say something else. But he shook his head, stood and left the room, mumbling something about putting on a shirt and shoes before we went shopping. I finished the rest of my breakfast without tasting it, then stood looking out the window and sipping coffee for a while. When I felt like enough time had passed for him to get himself together again, I followed him into the bedroom.

Chapter Four

Eric wanted to walk downtown instead of riding the bus. I was a little worried about him walking after he'd been so sick the night before, but he swore he felt back to normal after a good night's sleep and some food. So I gave in and we walked. He'd taken the bandage off his forehead, and the giant bruise caused more than a few double-takes from people we passed on the street. After the way he'd acted the night before, I was afraid he'd take offense at people staring and put someone's lights out for them. Either he didn't notice or didn't care, though, and that was fine with me.

It was a gorgeous June day, warm and breezy, the kind that makes you smile whether you want to or not. The tie-dye set played their bongos in Pritchard Park, tourists roamed from shop to shop, families sat on the benches eating ice-cream. Even the Goth kids were out, sweating in their black clothes. By the time we got to the shops downtown, Eric was laughing and relaxed and we were talking nonstop. It was amazing. I hadn't even known him a whole day yet, but it felt like we'd known each other forever.

We only had to hit a few stores to find all the clothes Eric needed. And I had to talk him into getting as much as he did. Some people have this vision of gay guys as fashion slaves, and I can't say I don't know some of those, but Eric definitely wasn't the fashionable type. Not that I have any room to talk since I'm pretty much a jeans-and-T kind of guy myself. I'm Liberace compared to Eric though. He was honestly puzzled when I suggested that he might want more than the one pair of jeans and couple of faded shirts he was going to buy at the Salvation Army thrift store.

"What's wrong with these?" He held them up and inspected them with a frown.

"Nothing. Well, actually, they're kinda ratty. That's not it, though. The thing is, don't you think you'll need more clothes than just that?"

"What for? I've still got my other clothes; they just need washing, is all." He stood blinking those big blue eyes just as innocently as you please, and I had to laugh.

"Eric, you're gonna want to get a job, aren't you? If you're staying in Asheville? You'll probably need something nicer than what you already have for that. And wouldn't you get tired of wearing the same thing all the time?"

"No. I mean, no, I don't get tired of wearing the same thing. One less thing you have to think about in the morning. But I see your point about getting a job." He sighed. "All right, you win. Make me beautiful."

As if I could improve on perfection, I thought.

Two consignment shops, one drug store, and a major clearance sale later, we headed for home loaded with several bags of clothes, shoes, and other supplies. Eric flatly refused to let me pay for anything. He insisted on buying it all himself, and even spent his last few dollars on a case of beer.

I paid for the bus so we wouldn't have to walk all the way home with all the stuff.

"You didn't have to get that beer, you know," I said for about the thirtieth time as we got off the bus and started walking the two blocks to my apartment.

"Fuck, don't you ever shut up? I wanted to. You gave me a place to stay, you took care of me, fed me...I owe you, man."

"You don't owe me anything. I helped you 'cause you needed someone. And I want you to stay. I like having you around."

He sighed. "Ben, if you don't stop whining about the fucking beer right now, I'm gonna gag you with one of these stupid shirts you made me buy."

"They're not stupid."

"Don't change the subject."

"I'm not!"

"Are." He grinned at me. "Don't make me get rough with you, boy."

That actually sounded like fun to me. But I didn't say that, since I wasn't sure how he'd take it. I dropped the bags I was carrying and held my hands up in mock surrender.

"Okay, I give. I'll shut up about the beer."

"Finally. First say 'thank you' like I know your mama taught you."

"Thank you," I echoed obediently.

"Very good!" He nudged the bags I'd dropped with his toe. "Now pick those up and let's go. This beer's getting heavy."

"Yessir." I picked up the bags and followed him on up the sidewalk to our building.

He pursed his lips and peered critically at me while I fished my keys out of my pocket. "Hmm. Smart, cute, trainable...there are definite possibilities here."

I tripped over my own feet and nearly fell flat on my face when I heard that. He laughed all the way to the front door. We got inside and his laughter stopped so fast it was like a switch being flipped. I followed his suddenly blank gaze and saw Janey was standing outside my apartment with her hand poised to knock.

"Ben!" she said. "Where were you?"

"We went shopping. Eric needed a few things."

Her eyebrows went up to her hairline, but she didn't say anything. "Well, I was just coming to remind you about work tonight."

"Thanks Janey, but I actually remembered this time."

"Good." She turned to Eric with what I called her Barbie smile, because it looked so fake. "Better today?"

"Yeah." He stared at her with undisguised hostility. The Barbie smile faded and she glared right back at him.

"What are you after?" she asked.

I glanced at Eric. The muscles in his jaw clenched tight and his eyes blazed. He'd managed to balance the beer case in one hand and was poised with his weight on the balls of his feet. He looked ready for a fight. This I definitely did not need.

"Janey!" I snapped. "Leave him alone. He's not after anything, all right? God."

She didn't take her eyes off Eric. "I think he can speak for himself. You were saying, Eric?"

"I wasn't saying anything to you." His voice was low and dangerous. "I don't owe you any explanations."

Her eyes darkened with anger. I stepped between them before things could go any more wrong.

"Janey, just go." My voice sounded weary. "We'll talk later, okay?"

"You better damn well believe we will." She shot one more murderous glare at Eric, then turned on her heel and stormed into her apartment.

I stared after her for a moment. Janey and I had been friends forever, and I hated it when we fought like this, but it had happened before and we always got past it.

I turned back to Eric. He'd relaxed some, but he still stood in a way that said he was ready to strike pretty damn fast if he had to.

"Sorry, man." I unlocked the door. "She's really great once you get to know her; she's just not easy to get to know."

"I can see that." He set the beer on the kitchen counter. "But I guess I can't say anything, huh?"

I shrugged. "I know you have your reasons, even if I don't know exactly what they are. Janey's the same way, you know. I think the two of you would get along really well if you'd take the time to make friends with each other."

"What makes you think we'll ever be friends? She's made it pretty clear that she doesn't want me around you."

"She'll come around." I dropped the bags in the bedroom and sat down on the bed. "We're best friends. She'll give you a chance, for me."

"I hope so. I don't want to come between you."

He sat down beside me, near enough that I could feel his heat. We stared at each other and my head started to whirl. He was so close that the urge to pull him to me and kiss him was almost overwhelming. The look in his eyes said that maybe he wanted it too. But I couldn't be sure, and I didn't want to scare him off. So I fought my rising desire with everything I had and managed to force myself to my feet again.

"I, uh, I have to get ready for work. Um, do you wanna come with me? You can, if you want."

"Naw, that's okay. I'll just stay here and watch TV."

"Okay, that's fine. I'll bring home some pizza for dinner, how's that? The restaurant where I work has the best pizza in town."

"Oh, man, that's perfect! I hate to ask, but can you get vegetarian?"

"Sure, I always do. I'm a vegetarian too."

He laughed. "Damn, I sure lucked out, didn't I? Me rooming with a carnivore never works out."

"Boy, did you ever come to the right city. I bet we have more gay vegetarians than any other place in the Southeast."

"Cool." He gazed up at me with a smile. "I think I'm gonna like it here."

"You will," I agreed. "I'm gonna grab a quick shower, then I have to go. Sure you'll be all right here alone?"

He rolled his eyes. "Yes, Mom, I'll be fine. Go on."

"Okay, okay." He waved a hand impatiently at me and I grinned.

The thought of him lounging on the bed in the next room while I showered turned me on. My imagination conjured images of him climbing into the shower with me, pressing his naked body against mine, kissing me, touching me… You can guess what that led to. It didn't take me long to come with those sorts of pictures in my head.

Eric was sprawled on his stomach on the bed watching TV when I emerged. I'd forgotten to get any clothes out before showering so I wasn't wearing anything but a towel. He looked up and flashed an evil grin at me.

"You wear that to work?" he teased. "What sort of restaurant is this?"

"Ha, ha. You should be a comedian. I don't usually bring clothes into the bathroom with me. I just forgot, is all."

He studied the TV screen with intense concentration while I pulled on underwear and discarded the towel. Once I had that much on, he stopped pretending to watch TV and rolled on his side to watch me dress. I had to resort to mental pictures of naked grandmas to keep a hard-on at bay.

"What's so fascinating?" I finally had to ask.

He smiled. "Just picking up some fashion tips."

"Smart ass." I pulled on my shoes and grabbed my wallet. "Okay, I'm off. I don't have to close tonight, but it'll still be kind of late. 'Bout nine-thirty, hope you don't mind waiting that long to eat."

"No problem." He stretched like a cat and let his head hang over the edge of the bed. He gave me an upside down grin and my heart stopped for a second. I wondered if he even knew how fucking sexy he was.

"See you later."

"Yeah, see you. Go on and lock the door behind me, I've got my keys."

I left and waited for the click of the lock before knocking on Janey's door. She was wearing a scowl that looked like it'd been stamped permanently on her face. She didn't even glance at me. Mike gave me a questioning look as we followed Janey's rigid back out to the car.

"What's up?" he whispered.

"She didn't say anything?"

"Nope."

I sighed. If she hadn't told Mike about the fight, that meant it was worse than I'd thought. "We kind of got in an argument earlier."

"Over Eric, right?"

"Yeah. She really hates him, dude."

"Hey, you know how she is, Ben. Give her a while. He doesn't seem that bad to me."

"He's not. He's a lot like her, matter of fact. And his reasons are just as good as hers."

Mike stared thoughtfully at me. "You know she worries about you. You give yourself so easily, and she just doesn't get that. She's scared of losing you like she lost her brother."

"I know. But I'm not Alan. He had problems before that woman ever came along."

"Yeah, but you know as well as I do that logic's got nothing to do with it. Alan's suicide messed her up more than she likes to let on."

"Don't I know it."

Alan had been twenty-five and Janey seventeen when he fell in love with Rhonda, a woman he'd met at church. They'd had a whirlwind romance and got married within a month of meeting each other. Janey had thought Rhonda hung the moon and stars and they hung out together a lot. Janey opened up to her like she never had with anyone else, other than me. Then less than a week after the honeymoon, Rhonda cleaned out Alan's bank account and disappeared without a trace. Alan shot himself in the head a few weeks later. Janey never got over it, and she never let anyone else get that close to her, except for Mike. She was as fiercely protective of Mike and me as a mama bear with her cubs. I understood it, but it was frustrating sometimes.

"God, would you guys hurry up?" Mike and I glanced at each other and hurried to the car where Janey stood fuming with impatience.

We rode to Marco's in silence. Mike dropped Janey and me off in front then headed to his own job as manager of the Alley Kat. If the ride over was tense, our shift at the restaurant was even worse. Everyone there could feel Janey's anger and stayed the hell out of her way, me included.

It worried me that she was so furious with me over Eric. I mean it's not like it was the first time I'd ever taken in someone that needed a place to stay. It wasn't even the first time I'd ever struck up a relationship of some sort with someone I'd helped out. A couple of them were still friends of mine, and she was even friends with one girl that she'd hated when she first met her. But I'd never seen her this angry with so little reason. It was distracting as hell, and I kept screwing up orders because I was so worried I couldn't concentrate.

By the time nine o'clock rolled around and my shift was over, I felt wrung out and irritable. I put in an order for an extra-large veggie pizza to go, and sat down in the break room to wait. Janey came shuffling in a few minutes later. I ignored her.

"Hey, Ben?"

"What?" I crossed my arms and glared at her.

She sighed. "Look, I don't blame you for being mad, but I wish you'd try to see my side of it."

"Well, why don't you tell me what your side is, Janey? Because I'm fucked if I know why you're so pissed at me."

She bit her lip and I was startled to see tears gathering in her eyes. I jumped up and hugged her.

"Janey, come on, what's wrong?" I stroked her hair and she relaxed a little.

"I'm sorry, Ben." She sniffled against my chest. "It's just, I know this Eric guy is trouble. I just know it, I can feel it. And you're falling for him, and I'm scared he's gonna hurt you."

I laughed. "What are you talking about? I'm not falling for him. I mean I like him, and he's definitely a babe, but we're just friends." I wished it was more, but right then I wasn't sure it was, or ever would be. And I was sure I wasn't in love with him. Lust and love are not the same thing. "You're worrying over nothing, Janey."

She shook her head. "No, I'm not. You may not be ready to admit it, but I know that look. You're falling for him, all right. I love you, and I don't want you to get hurt. I'm scared for you."

I lifted her chin so I could look her in the eye. "I'm a big boy. I can take care of myself. No matter what happens with Eric, I'll be fine. You're not going to lose me like you lost Alan. And we are always gonna be best friends, no matter what."

She smiled. "I know that. And I know I'm overprotective. I know you're not gonna…well, that you're not like Alan was. I know that. It's just hard to remember sometimes when I see you doing something stupid."

I laughed. "We'll have to agree to disagree on the 'stupid' part. But I'd like you to give Eric a chance, okay? He's a lot like you, you know. I think you'd like him if you got to know him."

She regarded me silently for a while. "Okay. I'll give him the benefit of the doubt. For you. But if he ever hurts you, he's toast!"

"I'll be sure and tell him that." I grinned at her, she grinned back, and things were back to normal again.

Chapter Five

Mike was relieved when he heard that Janey and I had made up. "Good! You have no idea how miserable life with that woman is when you guys are fighting, man."

She gave him an evil look and I laughed. The ride back home was definitely more relaxed than the ride to work, and my irritable mood was gone by the time I unlocked the door and let myself into my apartment.

I was just about to holler that I was home, when I heard something that stopped the words in my throat. Eric had found my acoustic guitar and was playing a song I didn't know. It was so beautiful that I was afraid to even breathe because I didn't want to break its spell. Then he started singing, and I had to set the pizza down before I dropped it. His voice was gorgeous, low and powerful and sexy as hell.

I kicked my sneakers off and padded over to the bedroom door. Eric was sitting cross-legged on the bed with his eyes closed and my guitar in his lap. He didn't seem to know I was there. The song's emotions flowed across his face as he sang, and I was captivated. I don't think I even blinked until his fingers plucked the final notes and the sounds faded away.

For a minute I couldn't move or talk. Then he set the guitar down with a deep sigh and I could breathe again.

"That was beautiful."

He jumped to his feet and crouched into fighting stance before I knew what was happening. When he saw it was just me, he let out a long breath and sat back down again.

"Fuck, you scared me. I didn't hear you come in."

"I figured. Sorry, I didn't mean to spook you like that."

He smiled. "It's okay. It's your place, after all. You should be able to come in any time without having to announce yourself."

"What was..."

I didn't get any further than that.

"Hey, where's the pizza? I'm starved!" He jumped up without waiting for me to finish my sentence and practically ran into the kitchen.

I followed him, puzzled. Why the hell didn't he want me to know what song he was playing? He had to know that's what I was about to ask. I shrugged and decided to try again later.

"Oh, man, that looks great!" He smiled at me as I trailed into the kitchen. He already had the box open and was piling pizza onto two plates. I grabbed two beers out of the fridge and handed him one, then took the loaded plate he held out to me.

We ended up sprawled on the floor of the bedroom, listening to CDs and talking while we ate. It didn't take us long to find out that we had similar tastes in lots of things: movies, books, music. We'd both seen Star Wars more than fifty times, and we both owned everything Clive Barker had ever written. And I was thrilled to find out that he was as big a Beck fan as me.

"Man's a fucking genius," Eric declared around a mouthful of pizza.

"Hell, yeah. Hot little piece of ass too."

"Dude, he's straight."

"Hey, I never converted a straight boy before, maybe he could be the first. I'd sure as hell like to give it a try."

Eric snorted with laughter. "Groupie!"

"Don't tell me you wouldn't do him."

He shrugged and grinned. "Maybe."

"Maybe, my ass."

He looked me up and down. "I'll think it over." He waggled his eyebrows at me and I blushed when I realized what he meant.

"You're too fucking cute when you blush like that." He laughed.

"Oh, so you do that on purpose, do you?" I reached over and grabbed my fourth beer out of the case we'd eventually brought into the bedroom with us. "See, now, you shouldn't have told me that, 'cause now it's not gonna work anymore. Your evil plans are foiled, bro."

"So you wouldn't blush if I told you you look so much like Beck that if you only had blue eyes, I'd jump your bones right now?"

"Nope. Because you're a dirty liar if you say that." I shook my head and gave myself a mental pat on the back for managing to not turn twelve shades of red.

"Fine, don't believe me." He grabbed himself another beer and cracked it open. "But it's true."

His eyes met mine and suddenly the air crackled. I could feel the attraction between us like a line of fire. He wanted me as much as I wanted him. His desire was plain on his face. The knowledge sent a thrill through my bones. I set my plate down and slid closer to him. Fear and want mingled in his eyes as he reached out to touch my cheek. My breath hitched in my chest.

"Eric..."

"No," he whispered. He closed his eyes and shrank away. "I, I'm sorry, I can't. I just can't."

I swallowed my heart back down. "Hey, it's okay. It's...it's the beer. I don't know about you, but drinking makes me friendly, you know?"

He opened his eyes and pierced me with that stare of his. "It's not the beer, and you damn well know it."

I took a deep breath. "Yeah, you're right. It's not. Look, I'm attracted to you, okay? I know it isn't easy for you to get close to people, and I didn't want to say anything 'cause I didn't want to make you uncomfortable. But just now, I thought that, that...hell, it's okay if you don't feel that way about me, you know. We're both adults here, I can handle it. Doesn't change anything. I still want to be friends, and you can still stay here, and..."

"Ben," he interrupted. "You didn't imagine it. I wanted to kiss you just then. It's not the first time I wanted that either. You really don't have any idea how beautiful you are, do you?" He smiled bitterly. "The hell of it is, if I didn't like you so damn much, I think I might've done it."

My head swam and I steadied myself with a hand on the floor. "Wh -- what...I mean, why..."

He laughed. The sound was sharp and jagged as broken glass. "You don't have a clue how fucked up I really am. Sometimes I think the hole I'm in, is so fucking deep I'll never be able to climb out again, no matter how hard I try or how much hell I go through trying to straighten myself out. You don't need to deal with that."

I stared hard at him. It seemed perfectly clear to me that he thought he'd gone too far and that he was planning to leave.

"Don't go, Eric." He paled but kept quiet. "I know I don't need to deal with it. But I want to. I want to help. I like you. Yeah, I'm attracted to you, but more than that, I want to be your friend. I don't know what's happened to you, but whatever's broken in there..." I laid a hand gently over his heart, "I want to help you fix it."

He stared at me with wide eyes, and I could see the struggle going on inside him. "We barely know each other. It scares me that I feel so comfortable with you. It's so easy to talk to you, it feels so good to be around you, and it just...scares me."

"Why, Eric? Tell me."

He was silent for so long that I thought he wasn't going to answer me. Then he took my hand in his and looked at me with determination in his eyes.

"You know the song I was playing before?"

The apparent change of subject startled me, but I kept quiet. Whatever he had to say, he needed to say it in his own way, in his own time.

"It was gorgeous," I said, truthfully enough.

"I wrote that for someone." He spoke barely above a whisper. "Someone I loved. Playing it helps me, when the memories get to be too much."

I squeezed his hand. "Tell me about him."

He closed his eyes and smiled. "I met him in Mobile, at the museum where I was working. I led tours there during the day and played in a club a few blocks away at night. Jason was new in town and was seeing all the sights." He laughed. "He asked me about a million questions during the tour, then after it was over he asked if I would mind showing him around the city. Of course I said yes. God, he had the most beautiful smile. I was in love before the day was out."

He opened his eyes again, but he didn't seem to see anything except pictures of the past in his mind. I held his hand and kept quiet. After a minute he started talking again.

"He moved in with me about a week later. We did everything together. He played the piano, and we started playing together at the club where I worked. He was like a part of me that I hadn't known was missing. I'd never felt that way about anyone, not ever. No one had ever gotten so close to me before. It happened so fast. It was like we had an instant connection. I loved him more than I've ever loved anybody, and he felt the same way about me."

His eyes focused on me. "That's why it scares me how easy it is to be with you, Ben. Because that's how it was with Jason. We're not in love, but I think we're friends at least, and it's weird how much talking to you feels like talking to him. I don't think I could stand it if anything happened to you."

"Like what? What happened to Jason?"

He drew a deep, shaky breath. "He, uh…he died. He, he was in a…a car crash, and he died."

"Jesus, Eric. I'm sorry."

He gave me an anemic smile. "I'm being stupid, huh?"

"No, you're not," I assured him. "The hardest thing in the world is losing someone you love, and it just makes it worse when it's so sudden, and so violent." An agonized look passed over his face and was gone before I could decide what it meant. "You can't help it if your mind makes those sorts of connections between the past and the present. But Eric, that's the risk you take when you make friends, or when you fall in love. There's always the chance that something's gonna happen, that you might get hurt. Sure, it's scary. But isn't it worth it? Would you trade your time with Jason for anything, even the guarantee of never getting hurt?"

He shook his head. "No. It hurts to remember, but I wouldn't give it up. Jason was the best thing I ever had."

I took both of his hands in mine. "Eric, I know it's hard for you to let someone really get to know you. I want to be your friend. Maybe more than that, if you want. You can take your time, I'm not gonna push you. We can take it as slow as you want. But I think a really good friend is worth the risk, don't you?"

He laughed. "Yeah, yeah I do. Damn, how the fuck do you do that?"

I frowned, puzzled. "Do what?"

"You make me want to talk to you. You make me feel...safe. Yeah. I feel safe with you." He stared solemnly at me. "I haven't felt safe with anybody in a long time."

I smiled at him. "Then I'm glad you feel like that with me."

We sat there gazing at each other, and I wanted more than anything to pull him into my arms and kiss him until he forgot to be afraid, or angry, or sad. It took everything I had to not do it. I just couldn't let him down by giving in to my desire. Suddenly a thought struck me, and I knew how I could help him.

"I've got an idea. You said you played in a club in Mobile, right?"

"Yeah."

"Well, Janey and I are in a band together, and we play every Friday night at The Alley Kat. Mike's the manager there, and he and the owner have been looking for someone to play and sing every night before the main act. I think you'd be perfect."

His jaw dropped open. "Whoa, you serious?"

"Hell, yeah. If what I heard earlier is any indication, they'd be falling all over themselves to hire you."

He stared silently at me for a long time. "Wow," he said finally. "I don't know what to say."

"Say you'll go for it. You can go with us tomorrow night and play for Mike and Tamara, she's the owner. You can play before they open up. I'll talk to Mike in the morning and let him know. So what about it? Will you do it?"

"I-I…fuck yeah, I'll do it!"

He grinned like a little kid and I laughed. "Great! Man, I can't wait to see their faces when they hear you sing!"

He burst out laughing and fell backward onto the carpet. "Shit, this is un-fucking-believable! I mean I wanted to find work here singing, but I never thought I'd even get an interview this soon, you know?" He propped himself up on an elbow and gave me a smile that melted my insides into a sticky little puddle. "Thanks, Ben."

I grinned a stupid, happy grin at him. "Hey, anything I can do."

He stood, stretched, and yawned. "I'm tired. Let's get all this picked up then get some sleep, huh?"

"Sounds like a plan. I'm pretty beat myself."

He held a hand down. I took it and he pulled me to my feet. For a second we stood there, staring at each other. He leaned toward me just a little and I stopped breathing. If he'd moved those last few inches and kissed me, I think I'd have died of heart failure. I wasn't sure whether to be disappointed or relieved when he blinked, shook his head, and pulled away from me.

We picked up the plates and beer cans and put away the leftover pizza, then took turns in the bathroom taking care of business before bed. I started to pull the extra pillow and blanket onto the floor and he stopped me with a hand on my arm.

"You're not sleeping on the floor again. My turn this time."

I shook my head. "I don't mind, really. I like the floor."

He grinned. "You're the worst liar in the world. Come on, I'll feel awful if I keep chasing you out of your own bed. I've slept in worse places than your floor, believe me."

I was getting ready to argue when I had a thought. He might not go for it, but I had to try.

"Hey, you know we could always share the bed. There's plenty of room."

His eyebrows shot up. "You wouldn't mind?"

"Not if you don't. It's okay if you don't want to, you know, but I wish you would. Because I'm not letting you sleep on the floor."

He smiled. "Okay, then. We'll share."

"Good. And don't worry, I'll keep my hands to myself."

He laughed, but as we climbed into the bed and I switched off the light, I could've sworn he looked disappointed.

Chapter Six

When I woke up the next morning, it was nearly ten and Eric was already up. He was in the kitchen, trying to make coffee quietly so he wouldn't wake me. It made me smile. I kicked off the tangle of covers, stood and stretched, then pulled on a pair of shorts and wandered into the kitchen.

"Hey," I said.

Eric turned and smiled at me. "Hey. Did I wake you up?"

"Naw. I'm usually up by this time anyhow."

"Do you have to go to work today?"

"Nope. It's Friday, I don't work Marco's on Friday since I play at The Alley Kat Friday nights."

"Oh, yeah. I forgot today was Friday." He bit his lip and studied the linoleum under his bare feet.

"Nervous?"

He laughed. "Yeah. Been a while since I played for an audience."

I leaned against the counter beside him, shoulder to shoulder. He raised his head and I could see all the what-ifs in his eyes.

"Hey, anybody would be nervous, but you're gonna be great. You'll see. Just relax and let it all come back to you."

He smiled. "I'll try."

"Good. So, what do you wanna do today? We've got most of the day free."

"Oh, um…don't know. Why don't we just hang out and watch TV or something? Or maybe go to a movie? If there's anything playing early enough, that is."

"Let's go to Second Sight, that's perfect!"

"Second Sight?"

"Yeah, it's a little movie theater just a couple of blocks from here. They have dollar matinees every day. What about it, you wanna go?"

He grinned. "Sure, it sounds great. What's playing?"

"Hang on, let me see." I rummaged around the shelves next to the bed until I found that week's copy of *Mountain Xpress*, then flipped to the movie section. "Oh, man, they're playing *Return of the Living Dead* this week! Cool."

"Oh, I fucking love that movie, man."

"Me too," I agreed. "Okay, let's do it!"

He laughed, then sobered so suddenly if left me reeling.

"What is it?"

He looked stricken. "I don't have any money left, Ben. Damn, I didn't even think of that."

"Shit, Eric, that's no big deal. I've got enough."

"But…"

"But nothing," I interrupted. "Look, if you really want to get your shorts in a wad over a dollar, you can pay me back after you get the job at The Alley Kat. But I want to go to the fucking movie, so we're damn well going."

He stared openmouthed at me for a minute, then burst out laughing. "Okay, boss, you win. Damn, you do have a way with words."

I crossed my arms and gave him my best smug look. "I know."

By noon, we'd polished off the coffee, taken turns showering, and were ready to head to the movies. I ran across the hall to talk to Mike before we left. He sat and listened silently while I gushed about Eric's talent.

"Wow," Mike said when I finally stopped talking, "I'm anxious to hear him now. If he's as good as you say, he'll be perfect for this job."

"He is. Wait 'til you hear him Mike, he's amazing."

"Who?"

I turned to see Janey standing behind me with her hair in a towel and Mike's robe wrapped around her.

"Eric. I found out he used to sing and play guitar at a club in Mobile. I heard him last night, and he's incredible. He's gonna try for the job at The Alley Kat."

Janey raised her eyebrows. "Oh? Well, okay then. Good. Hope he gets it."

I smiled at her. "Thanks, Janey."

She shrugged. "I promised I'd give him a chance. So I am." She turned and went back into the bathroom, swinging the door closed behind her.

Mike and I looked at each other and grinned. Janey was a force of nature; you either dealt with her on her terms, or you got the hell out of the way. We both understood that.

"Come over at four," Mike said. "I'll call Tamara before we go and tell her we've got a candidate for the position."

"Thanks, Mike. See you later."

I pulled him into a hug, then went back across the hall to my own place, where Eric waited.

* * *

Three hours later, the movie was over and Eric and I were discussing our favorite parts as we walked home.

"The end," he said. "I mean come on, dropping the bomb on the zombies, then the smoke seeding the rain clouds with that zombie-making chemical and the rain falling on all the cemeteries? That's fucking brilliant."

"Maybe, but it's depressing as hell. I vote for the part where the zombies eat the cops then call for more on the radio."

He laughed. "'Send more cops!' Yeah, that was genius. But I still vote for the ending. That's what would really happen, you know."

"Fine, be that way. Anybody ever tell you, you think too much?"

He gave me a sly sidelong smile. "All the time."

We grinned at each other and I felt a warm glow inside me. I've always gotten along with most people and made friends easily, but being with Eric felt so natural that it made all my previous relationships seem like hard work. I couldn't figure why that was either. Eric was cynical, suspicious, hot-tempered, and extremely prickly, and he had a truckload of emotional baggage. But everything between us clicked perfectly. It was weird and thrilling and a little unnerving.

We got back home just in time to change clothes and grab a bite of leftover pizza before Mike came knocking at the door. I hollered at him to come on in and he sauntered into the kitchen a few seconds later.

"You guys ready?" he asked.

"Yeah, all set," I said. "Eric?"

He nodded. "Ready as I'll ever be. Hey, Mike, I appreciate you letting me audition, man, thanks."

"No problem," Mike said. "I'm looking forward to it. You should've heard how Ben was talking about you; he thinks you're the reincarnation of Elvis and John Lennon both at once."

Eric shot an amused glance at me. The playful glint in Mike's eyes told me he'd said that on purpose just to embarrass me. I could've cheerfully killed him.

"You may be a smart-ass, Mike, but you're not far off. Just wait, you'll see."

"Oh, great," Eric groaned. "Way to keep the pressure off, Ben."

Mike laughed. "Don't worry, we're not a tough audience. Well, I guess Tamara kind of is, but she's so nice you won't notice it. Relax, bro, you'll be fine."

"That's what I keep telling him," I said. "Okay, let me get my guitar and we can go."

Fifteen minutes later, Mike dropped Janey, Eric, and me off in front of the bar and went on to the private lot down the street to park. Eric studied the sign outside the door with interest. His jaw dropped open when he got to the listing for Friday night. He whooped with laughter. I waited patiently for him to calm down and ask me about it. Janey hoisted her fiddle case under her arm, cocked an eyebrow at me, and went inside without a word.

"Oh shit," Eric gasped when he finally got the giggles under control. "Naked Cello? The name of your band is Naked Cello?"

"Yep. Ask me how we came up with that, go on."

"Okay, I'll bite. How the fuck did you come up with that name?"

"Oh, it's a long story, you don't wanna hear."

He gave me a dark look as we pushed the carved wooden door open and went inside. "Tease."

"Uh-huh."

"I'm really curious now, you know."

"I know."

"You're evil."

"I know that too."

He growled in frustration. "I give up. You're not gonna tell me, are you?"

I laughed. "It really is kind of a long story. It involves the members of our band, too much tequila, Janey's old cello, and a whole lot of finger paint. The rest is a little hazy, to tell you the truth."

He regarded me with an amused grin. "I'm not even telling you the sort of mental picture I'm getting right now."

"Oh, I can imagine. And you'd be more or less right."

We both laughed, and I felt electricity jump between us when our eyes locked. His gaze thickened and I knew he felt it too. What neither of us seemed to know was what to do about it. He wasn't ready to act on our mutual attraction, and I didn't want to push him. So we were sort of stuck. We stood there, staring at each other, not saying any of the things we wanted to say. Mike saved it from becoming a seriously uncomfortable moment by walking up right then with Tamara beside him.

"Eric," he said, "this is Tamara Binns; she owns this dive. Tamara, this is Eric...sorry, what's your last name again?"

"Green. It's Eric Green," Eric answered. I realized with a shock that I'd forgotten all about asking him his last name. Freaky.

"Eric's here to audition for the opening act position," Mike continued.

"Nice to meet you, Eric." Tamara smiled as she shook Eric's hand. "Mike tells me that Ben was very impressed with you."

Eric smiled. "That's what he says. I hope I can live up to that."

Tamara laughed. "I'm sure you will. Ben won't let on, but he's quite a talented musician himself, and he has a wonderful ear. He's never wrong about talent. I've learned to trust his opinion."

Eric glanced over and raised his eyebrows at me. "I'll do my best. I'd sure love to get back on stage again."

"How long's it been since you've worked?" Tamara asked.

"Um, a month or so since the last time I played. Before that it was off and on for a few months, just one-night gigs here and there. I was injured pretty badly nine months ago and spent a long time in the hospital and then in rehab. But before being injured I played six nights a week at a nightclub in Mobile, Bienville Tavern. Played there for...oh, a couple of years I guess."

Tamara nodded thoughtfully. "Okay. Well, whenever you're ready the stage is already set up and we're ready to listen."

She smiled at him and he nodded. "All right, well, I guess I'm ready now. Ben, can I use your guitar?"

"Sure." I handed it over. Eric smiled nervously at me and I laid a hand on his arm and leaned close to whisper in his ear, "It's okay, you'll be great. Just sing to me and don't worry about Mike and Tamara. That always helps me when I'm nervous."

He turned his head as I pulled away again, and my knees nearly went when his cheek brushed against mine. "Thanks, Ben," he said softly. He took my hand and pressed it for a second, then headed for the stage before I could make a total idiot out of myself by jumping him right then and there. I fell into the nearest chair and tried to gather my scattered wits.

"Hey, Ben."

The voice sounded right in my ear, and I about jumped out of my skin before I realized it was Malcolm. He pulled up a chair and sat down next to me, grinning.

"Malcolm, you jackass, you about scared the pants off me."

"Yeah, you wish," he said. "So, he's good, huh?"

For a second I got what Malcolm was saying all mixed up with the dirty thoughts in my head and almost told him I didn't know yet, but I figured so. Then it hit me what he was talking about.

"Yeah. Just listen, you'll see."

Malcolm gave me a skeptical look, but he settled back in his chair and turned his attention to the stage as Eric approached the mic.

Eric stood with head bowed and eyes closed. When he started plucking the guitar strings and his voice soared through the room, I forgot about everything else and gave myself up to the beauty of the music. It washed over me like summer sunshine and cool water, making me feel light and peaceful. I never wanted it to end.

Through the whole thing, I kept my eyes glued to Eric's face. Up there on stage, playing and singing, he was completely in his element. The hard shell he hid behind vanished when he sang, and his face became a mirror for all the fear and joy and sorrow and love of life that he didn't want to show any other time. It was beautiful. Every note he played pulled me in deeper, and by the time the song ended and he stepped back, that was it. I was in love.

The room was silent for a heartbeat, then we all broke into spontaneous applause. Eric smiled as he came down off the stage. His gaze caught mine and my heart stopped. His eyes shone, his cheeks were flushed, and he couldn't seem to stop grinning. It was the first time I'd seen him look so happy. I stood and walked over to him, and he gave me an oddly shy look before turning to Tamara.

"So," he said to her, "what do you think?"

Tamara shook her head. "Eric, that was absolutely beautiful. I've never heard it before, what's it called?"

"It doesn't really have a name yet," he answered. "I just wrote it this morning."

Tamara's green eyes widened in surprise. "Wow, that's pretty impressive. I think you've got the job. Mike?"

"Oh, yeah," Mike said. "No doubt."

Eric smiled hugely and shook Tamara's hand, then Mike's. "Thank you so much, this really means a lot to me."

"You can start whenever you like," Tamara said. "Is tomorrow too soon?"

"No, not at all, I'll be here."

"Great. Come on into my office, I have some paperwork for you to fill out."

"Okay, be right there."

Tamara headed off to her office. Eric stood bouncing on his toes and looking about twelve.

"God, this is fucking great!" he said. "I can't believe it!"

"Told you. I knew they'd want to hire you."

He stepped closer. "It wouldn't have happened without you. I can't even tell you how happy this makes me. Thank you, Ben."

I don't know what I would've said. Whatever it was vanished like a stray thought when Eric threw his arms around my neck and pulled me against him in a fierce hug. For a split second I was frozen. Then my arms went around his waist all by themselves, my temperature went up about ten degrees and I thought I could die happy right then. It seemed like forever and no time at all before he pulled away with a smile and followed Tamara to her office. I stood there grinning like an idiot until Malcolm came strolling over. He shook his head sadly.

"Ben," he said, "you have got it bad, bro."

I just shrugged and grinned even harder, too dazed to argue. Malcolm laughed.

"You gonna tell Eric?"

That brought me down pretty damn fast. "No."

"Why not?"

"He's not ready to hear something like that."

"What, is he on the rebound or something?"

"Not exactly. He's...well..." I didn't know how to explain without betraying Eric's confidence. He probably wouldn't appreciate me telling a bunch of people he didn't know about his attack and about his lover's death. "He's been through a lot. I can't really say anything else since it's not my place to tell his story. But trust me, he's not ready for a relationship right now."

"Okay. But Ben, don't leave it forever. He obviously likes you a lot; you both deserve a chance to see where it could go."

"I know. Gonna have to take it slow though."

Malcolm nodded. He shifted his weight and winced as he moved the knee Eric had kicked the other night.

"Hey Malcolm, what happened that night? With Eric, I mean."

Malcolm furrowed his brow in thought. "He came in and sat down at the bar and asked for a glass of water, so I gave it to him and forgot about him. Next thing I knew, people were yelling and stuff, and when I looked over to where he was sitting, Eric had punched that big guy in the stomach. I told Eric to leave, and he did. It's funny, he was furious, but he looked really scared too. Anyway, the other guy followed him outside. I was afraid someone was gonna get hurt, so I went out as soon as I got hold of Tamara to cover the bar for me. You know the rest."

"So what did the guy do to piss Eric off?"

Malcolm shrugged. "I didn't see. But some girl who was sitting next to him said that he was trying to pick Eric up. Said that Eric told the guy to fuck off, but he just laughed. Then she said the guy started touching him and he just flipped out."

"Malcolm!" Mike called from behind the bar. "Where's that extra case of Bailey's?"

Malcolm sighed. "Hang on, I'll look." He hurried off and I sat down to think. I already knew that Eric didn't like being touched unless he initiated it. And now I knew he definitely didn't like anyone coming on to him. Lots of people don't, I guess, but I thought his reaction was pretty extreme. Made me wonder about him even more than I already did.

I was so deep in thought that I didn't even notice that Eric had returned from Tamara's office. He stood grinning down at me for I don't know how long, before his presence finally registered.

"Hey," he said. "What planet were you on?"

"Sorry. I was just thinking."

"'Bout what?"

"Nothing much," I lied. "Let me buy you a drink to celebrate."

He smiled. "Okay."

I stood up and we headed for the bar, where Malcolm was busy setting up for the night.

"What'll it be?" I asked. "You like tequila?"

"Yeah, sounds great."

"Tequila it is, then," I answered as we sat down at the bar. "Hey, Malcolm!"

"Be with you in a sec," Malcolm called from under the bar. He rummaged around a little more, then reappeared looking mussed and sweaty, with the missing case of Bailey's in his hands. "I knew I had that around here someplace. Now, what'll you have?"

"Tequila," I said. "Shots, with lime."

"Coming right up," Malcolm said.

Eric watched him as he opened a fresh bottle and set two shot glasses and a plate of lime wedges in front of us. "Malcolm?" he said hesitantly.

"Yeah?"

"I'm sorry about the other night. I hope I didn't hurt you too bad."

Malcolm smiled. "The knee's still sort of tender, but that's all."

Eric bit his lip. "I don't usually do that sort of thing. That guy really pissed me off though, and when you grabbed my arm I just sort of acted on instinct. Sorry."

"Forget it," Malcolm said. "No major damage done. Looks like you banged your head pretty good though."

Eric laughed. "Yeah. Good thing black and purple are my colors."

"Like you'd know," I chimed in as I poured the tequila. "Calling you fashion challenged would be the understatement of the century."

He gave me an evil look. "You should talk." He tossed back his shot and bit into a lime wedge. He shuddered. "Oh, man, that's good."

"You move pretty quick in a fight," Malcolm said. "Looks to me like you've had some martial arts training, am I right?"

Eric nodded. "Black belts in three disciplines. I started when I was five and I liked it so much I kept at it, right up until I left Mobile."

"Wow, that's pretty impressive," I said.

He smiled at me. "I'll teach you, if you want."

"That would be way too cool."

"I run too," he added. "At least five miles every other day. You wanna come with me?"

"Don't know about that, man."

"Aw, come on. It's fun once you get used to it."

"Yeah, if you're a masochist maybe."

"Just try it once with me. I swear I won't make it too hard."

Too late, I thought. But I had to admit he was wearing me down.

"Okay," I said. "I'll go with you some time."

"Great."

I poured more tequila. We clinked our glasses together and tossed it back.

The bar opened about an hour later. Eric and I were both feeling pretty good by then. Mike and Janey joined us after a little while and we sat talking over the increasing noise of the crowd until nine o'clock rolled around. Janey glanced up at the clock, then stood and tugged on my sleeve.

"Time to go, Ben," she said. "You're still capable of playing, aren't you?"

"Oh, sure, no problem." I stood up and managed not to sway too much. Eric choked back a laugh.

"Okay then," Janey said. "Come on." She leaned over and kissed Mike, then grabbed my arm and pulled me with her. We took our places on stage with the rest of the band and launched into a hard and sweaty two-hour set.

It's a good thing we weren't trying out any new material that night, because I was hopelessly distracted. Eric and Mike sat at a small table near the stage, finishing off the tequila while we played. Eric's gaze caught mine and held it, and I played the whole set staring into his eyes. When it was over, I felt like I was waking up from a dream.

"Goddamn, that was fucking great!" Eric declared as we came down off the stage.

I plopped down into the chair next to him and mopped the sweat off my face with a napkin. "Thanks. Hey, can I have some of your water, Janey?" I grabbed her water bottle without waiting for an answer and guzzled half of what was left.

"Keep it," she said when I tried to hand it back to her. She turned to Eric. "Forgot to tell you before, I loved your song earlier. It was gorgeous." Her eyes held a grudging but genuine respect.

He gave her a loopy, tequila-fueled grin. "Thanks!"

Mike glanced at Eric and back at me, and smiled. "Hey, Janey can you come help me with something?"

She started to say something, then the light bulb went on over her head. She frowned, but got up and went with Mike.

I cleared my throat. "It really was a beautiful song. You said you wrote that this morning? Really?"

He nodded. "Yeah. In my head. I hardly ever write them down."

"Pretty amazing. I can't write in my head."

"I wrote it for you, Ben."

I choked on a mouthful of water. "What? You did what?" I croaked once the coughing stopped.

"I wrote it for you," he repeated. "You didn't have to help me. I sure gave you plenty of reasons not to. But you did it anyway. Nobody's ever done anything like that for me before. So I wrote that song for you, because it was all I could give you."

"Wow," I managed once I could make myself talk again. "I don't know what to say. Wow."

He gave me a smile that warmed me right through. "Don't say anything." He took my hand and laced his fingers through mine.

We sat there talking for probably another hour. I'm not sure what we talked about, because the feel of his hand in mine and his thigh pressed against me seemed much more important than anything either of us might say.

By the time we left the bar and said goodnight to Mike and Janey at the door of my apartment, my body ached all over with longing and I didn't know how I was going to get into bed with Eric and not molest him. The look in his eyes said that he was wondering the same thing.

We stripped down to boxers and T-shirts and brushed our teeth without saying a word. Eric turned off the light and we crawled under the covers. I could sense the warmth of his body only inches from mine, and it was all I could do to keep myself from reaching out and pulling him to me. It seemed like I lay there in mental agony forever. Then I felt him stir and a warm, callused hand slid up my arm. I gulped.

"Eric…"

"Shut up."

I shut up. The mattress creaked a little as he propped himself up on one elbow and leaned over me. His hair glinted in the faint light leaking around the closed curtains, but I couldn't see his face. I knew what he was going to do though. The rational part of my brain screamed at me to say something, anything, to stop him, because I knew it was too soon. But the rest of me was on fire, so I didn't say a word when he bent down and kissed me.

I reached up and cradled his face between my hands as he pulled back again. His gaze felt heavy, even in the dark. He laid a hand on my cheek and I practically purred.

"Goodnight, Ben," he whispered.

"'Night."

He pulled away and settled against his pillow. I lay there wide awake for a long time.

*   *   *

I must have drifted off at some point, because I woke with a start several hours later. At first I wasn't sure what had woken me. Then there was a grunt and a jerk from the other side of the bed. I sat up and leaned over Eric.

"Jason," he mumbled. "Jason, don't leave me..." He let out a heartbroken little sob that cut me like a razor. I wrapped my arms around him and held him spooned against me with his back against my chest, stroking his hair. After a few minutes, his trembling stopped and he lay quiet in my arms.

"Love you, Jason," he sighed in his sleep.

It hurt to hear that. Not only because of how much Jason's death still haunted him, but also because it was Jason he wanted and not me. It was totally unfair of me to be jealous of a dead man, but I couldn't help it. I closed my eyes and held Eric close, and let myself pretend that it was me he loved. Eventually the ache inside me eased a little and I fell asleep again.

Chapter Seven

When I woke up the next morning, Eric was curled around me with his face buried in my neck and one arm wound around my waist. It was cute as hell. I kissed his cheek, then untangled myself and went into the kitchen to make coffee. He padded in behind me just as it finished brewing a few minutes later. I poured us both a cup and we stood staring silently at each other.

"So," he said finally, "what's on for today? Anything?"

He had his blank face on, meaning he didn't want to talk about what had happened the night before. I decided to play it his way, for the time being.

"I'm working the lunch shift today at Marco's. I'll be back in plenty of time to go to The Alley Kat with you though."

He smiled. "I'm glad you're coming with me."

"Wouldn't miss it."

We fell silent again. He looked down at the floor, up at the ceiling, anywhere but at me. I waited. Finally he set his coffee on the counter and looked me in the eye.

"I meant it, you know," he said. "When I kissed you. I meant it."

"I know you did."

"Are we still friends?"

He looked so young and unsure right then. I set my cup down and took his hand.

"Of course we are," I assured him. "One kiss can't change that."

He bit his lip. "What about two?"

I swallowed. "Wh -- what?"

He stepped closer. "Would we still be friends if I kissed you again?"

"Yes," I whispered.

He pulled me against him and pressed his lips to mine. The kiss was light and quick and made me burn for more. Fear and desire radiated from him, so strong it felt like heat on my skin.

"Eric, you don't have to..."

He cut me off with a hand against my lips. "You talk too much."

He threaded one hand into my hair, pulled my face to his, and kissed me again. This time, his mouth opened and his tongue slid over mine. A hot wave of arousal roared over me. I wound both arms around his waist and melted into him.

I guess I got a little carried away. But I was so lost in the taste of his mouth and the feel of him in my arms that I couldn't think. Not an excuse, when I knew how skittish he was about being touched unexpectedly, but it's the only explanation I have for what I did. I slipped both hands inside his boxers to cup his butt in my palms.

He went rigid, then before I knew what was happening he'd broken out of my arms to huddle wild-eyed and panting against the opposite wall. For a second I couldn't figure out what had happened. Then it hit me like a brick between the eyes.

"Oh, shit, I'm sorry! Are you okay?"

He shook his head. "No. I don't know. Fuck!"

He kicked the wall so hard he knocked a hole in it. With his bare foot. If it hurt him, he didn't show it. When he turned to look at me, he looked so furious that I backed up.

"Eric? I'm really sorry, I shouldn't have touched you like that."

He laughed. The sound had a hysterical edge.

"Why not? Why shouldn't you be able to touch me exactly like that? I mean, fuck, if you're with someone and you're kissing him and you're both hard as a fucking rock, you should be able to touch each other however you want, right?"

He broke off and started pacing, both arms wrapped around himself. I watched, speechless. After a minute or so, he stopped and skewered me with his eyes.

"If it was anyone else but me you were with, you'd be in bed together right now. It's not your fault, Ben. It's me. I'm the one who's so fucked up that no one can touch me, even when I want it so bad I can't stand it. You deserve better."

Before I could say a word, he turned and strode into the bedroom. I could hear drawers opening and closing, and I followed him with my mind full of fear. Sure enough, he'd dressed and was shoving his few belongings into a big plastic bag. I ran to him and grabbed both of his wrists. He went still.

"Let go."

"No. Not until you calm down and talk to me."

He looked at me with such sorrow in his eyes that it nearly ripped me apart.

"You just don't get it, do you? I can't be with you. Not now, maybe not ever. You want something I can't give you. You deserve somebody who can give you everything."

He twisted out of my grip, finished shoving his things into the bag, and started for the door. I followed him, feeling helpless and desperate.

"Please, don't leave," I begged. "Please. I may not know all your reasons, but I know you're not ready for anything physical yet, and I shouldn't have pushed you. I am so, so sorry. Please stay."

He turned, dropped the bag on the floor, and laid both hands on my cheeks. His thumbs caressed the corners of my mouth and I had to fight the urge to kiss him.

"I can't. Don't you understand? I want you so fucking bad it hurts, and I don't think I can stand to live here with you and never be able to touch you the way I want to. Do you really want me to be here, when we both want to be together but can't? It'll never work, Ben."

"Eric, we can find a way. I'll sleep on the floor, I'll…"

"No," he interrupted. "Look, it's better this way. We'll still see each other, and I hope we'll still be friends. But it can't be more than that. Not for me. Jason was my only chance, and he's gone, and I'm too fucked up to ever be with anyone again. I don't think I really believed that until now. But it's true. 'Bye, Ben."

He stepped back, picked up his bag, and was gone before I could recover. I stood there for a long time, staring at the door. Finally it started to sink in that he'd really left. I stumbled to the bed and lay down with my face buried in his pillow. His scent clung to the cloth of the pillowcase. I breathed it in, and that did it. I curled up and cried until I was empty.

For the first time ever, I called in sick to work. When Janey came knocking on the door, I yelled that I was sick and staying home, and to leave me alone. She yelled back that she knew better and I'd damn well better let her in and talk to her when she got home. I ignored her and she eventually left.

True to her word, she was back after work, pounding on my door so hard I thought she might actually knock it down. Finally, I got up with a sigh and opened the door. She shoved past me and stood glaring at me.

"Come on in, Janey." I shut the door behind her.

"What the hell's wrong with you? And don't give me that crap about being sick either."

I shuffled over to the chair and fell into it. "I did a terrible thing, Janey. I really, really fucked up."

"You? That's hard to believe."

"It's true. I went too far, and now he's gone."

She was about to say something scathing about Eric, I could tell. But she stopped and looked harder at me, and her face softened. She sat down on my lap, put her arms around my neck, and leaned her cheek against my hair.

"I'm sorry. Want to tell me about it?"

I did want to. Janey and I have our differences, but we've always been there for each other, and I knew she'd listen and help if she could. Wrapping my arms around her, I leaned my head on her shoulder.

"He kissed me," I began. "And we kept on kissing. It felt so good, you know? I was so turned on I couldn't think straight. And I touched him...I touched him in a way I shouldn't have."

"What did you do?"

I took a deep breath and made myself say it. "I put my hands inside his pants and...you know, groped him."

"You mean he didn't want you to? But he kissed you first."

"Yeah, but you know that doesn't mean anything."

"Okay, you're right. Well, I know you stopped when he said stop, though."

"He didn't, not exactly. He just...freaked out." I frowned and tried to think how to explain it to her. "The thing is, some things have happened to him, and they left pretty deep scars. He hasn't told me everything, but he told me enough before this happened for me to know better than to do what I did."

"I don't believe for a second that you forced yourself on him."

"I didn't. He wanted it too, he just can't handle it right now. When I touched him, he wasn't expecting it, and he panicked. He was so upset with himself, he just packed and left. He said I deserved better."

She sighed. "I think he's right, that you do deserve better. But," she continued before I could protest, "I know you. You don't want 'better,' whatever that is. You want Eric. You love him, don't you?"

I nodded against her neck. "What am I gonna do, Janey? I can't leave things like this."

"Tell him how you feel, Ben."

"I can't."

"Why not?"

I laughed bitterly. "I'm afraid I'll scare him away for good."

She sat in silent thought for a minute. "Maybe he just needs some time. Give him that time, and let him know you're there when he's ready."

I looked up into her eyes. "You're being awfully nice about this, considering how you feel about him."

She shrugged. "Doesn't matter how I feel, Ben. You're my best friend, and I love you. If being with Eric is what makes you happy, then I want that for you. And I may not like him much, but it's pretty obvious that he's crazy about you."

I grinned at her, then hugged her so hard she squealed. "I love you, Janey."

"So why are trying to squish me?" She giggled.

I laughed and let her go. She stood up. "You're going to hear Eric play tonight, right?"

"Yeah. I have to."

"Good. I'm going too. Come over, we'll all ride together."

"Okay." I got up to walk her to the door. "Hey, Janey?"

"Yeah?"

"Thanks for listening."

"You can always talk to me about anything. That's what best friends are for."

She hugged me, squeezed my hand, and left. I had to admit I felt better. She had a knack for putting things in perspective and making me see what I had to do. By the time I'd showered and dressed, my despair was gone. I loved Eric, and I was willing to wait for him. Hopefully, he could eventually feel something besides friendship for me. I had Jason's memory to compete with, but the biggest obstacle was Eric's mysterious past and the damage it had done to him. And I didn't know how to fight his past, because I didn't even know what it was.

Chapter Eight

Time passed, and my life settled into a new routine. At first, I went to The Alley Kat every night to hear Eric play. He always had a smile for me, and he never ignored me or gave me the cold shoulder. But it wasn't the same; he was more guarded than ever. After a while, we barely said more than 'hello' to each other. I could see it happening and hated it, but I couldn't stop it. No matter how hard I tried, I couldn't find a single chink in the wall he'd built around himself, and I started to lose hope.

Eventually, I stopped going to The Alley Kat altogether, except on Fridays, when I had to play. Mike told me that Eric was living in the little studio apartment above the bar, that he'd finally bought himself a guitar so he wouldn't have to keep borrowing, and that he was rapidly becoming one of the most popular acts in town. I was happy for him, but the distance between us was so painful that I could hardly be around him anymore. I missed him so much, and wished I could go back in time and relive that one fatal moment. I'd fucked everything up, and I would've given anything to change that.

On the surface, Eric's life had improved a lot since he'd first come to Asheville. He had a small but nice apartment in the middle of the city, he had a job doing what he loved, and he had the admiration and respect of everyone who heard him play. The funny thing was, he didn't seem nearly as happy as he should have. In fact, he looked as miserable as I felt. Two months after he'd moved out of my apartment, I could tell he'd lost weight and he wasn't sleeping much. The most telling thing, though, was his music. The peacefulness was gone from his songs, replaced by a quiet despair. They were still some of the most beautiful songs I'd ever heard, but it broke my heart to hear them.

My friends, of course, couldn't help but notice the change in me. I didn't mean to neglect them, but I just didn't have the energy to do anything beyond what was absolutely necessary. I went to work, practiced and played with Naked Cello, ate a little and slept less, and that was it. Mike was worried, and Janey was beside herself. She started letting herself into my apartment with the extra key, and I quit complaining about it once I realized she wasn't going to stop. She'd talk to me about little things while cooking me dinner or picking up the mess I couldn't be bothered with. Sometimes she'd just sit with me and hold my hand. Her presence comforted me, even though I couldn't ever bring myself to talk about Eric and how badly things had gone wrong.

Oddly enough, it was Malcolm who finally confronted me. We were friends, sure, but we'd never been the kind of friends who sat down and had long, heart-to-heart talks. Janey was that sort of friend to me; Malcolm wasn't. So I was pretty surprised when I walked into the bar one Friday night and he immediately pulled me into Tamara's office and shut the door.

"What do you want?" Not so long ago, I would've had some smart-ass remark to make. But now, I was just too tired.

"How long are you gonna do this, Ben?" Malcolm leaned against the desk, crossed his arms, and stared at me with challenge in his eyes.

"Do what?"

"This!" he repeated. "Moping around like someone shot your dog instead of getting off your ass and doing something about it. It's not like you."

I wanted to pretend I didn't know what he was talking about, but I couldn't do it. Pretending took energy I just didn't have anymore.

"Malcolm, there are some things you just can't fix. This is one of them."

"That's bullshit and you know it. Haven't you noticed that Eric's just as unhappy as you are? Or have you been too busy feeling sorry for yourself?"

I glared at him. He was starting to make me mad. The fact that he was most likely doing it on purpose didn't make any difference.

"Yeah, I've noticed. So what? In case you haven't noticed, he doesn't want anything to do with me."

"Oh, come on, you know that's not true. You could at least be civil to him. I know how you feel about him, Ben. Don't you think you can at least be his friend?"

That did it. I stood up so fast the chair fell over and clattered to the floor.

"His friend?" I shouted. "He won't let me be his fucking friend! He won't let me get close enough! And I can't just be that guy he says 'hi' to now and then! I love him, Malcolm. I tried to be patient. I would wait for him forever if he'd just give me something to go on, but he won't. I can't just stand around making polite small talk with him when I want so much more than that. It hurts too fucking much."

Malcolm stood still and silent during this outburst. Then when it was over and I sank down to the floor with my head in my hands, he knelt beside me and laid a hand on my shoulder.

"I know this is hard for you," he said. "But you can't sit back and wait for him. I don't know what his story is, but it's pretty obvious that he's not going to be able to take the initiative. It's up to you. You have to tell him how you feel, Ben. It's the only way."

I raised my head to look into Malcolm's calm, kind eyes. "I'm scared."

He nodded. "I know. But you have to try."

"I don't know if I can."

"You can. You're a lot tougher than you think you are, and I know you can do this. Now come on, Eric's gonna be playing in a few minutes."

He pulled me to my feet and we went back out into the bar. It was starting to get crowded. I looked around and finally spotted Eric sitting alone at a little table in the shadows at the back of the room.

He had a bottle of tequila in front of him, and he slammed back a shot as I watched. Something told me it wasn't his first drink of the evening, and it wouldn't be his last. He looked lost and broken, and suddenly it all seemed so clear to me. I'd thought all this time, that in spite of the attraction between us, he no longer wanted even friendship from me. That's probably what he told himself. But when I saw him sitting there, drinking alone in the dark, I knew it wasn't true. He needed me as much as I needed him, but he couldn't admit it even to himself because he didn't think he was worth my time. The second I realized that, I stopped being afraid. I went to him and sat down beside him.

He glanced over at me, threw back another shot, and refilled the glass. "Hi," he said. "Want some?"

He held the shot glass out to me. I shook my head. "No, thanks."

"Suit yourself. More for me." He drank it down and reached for the bottle again. I grabbed his wrist and he gave me a dangerous look.

"Eric, we need to talk."

"'Bout what?" His face was blank and empty.

"I have some things I need to say to you. Things I should've said a long time ago."

"Ben, whatever it is, doesn't matter now. Just leave it alone."

"I'm not gonna do that anymore. Eric, please, listen to me..."

He shook free of my grip and stood up. "I have to go."

"Eric..."

He turned his back on me and headed for the stage. I wanted to run after him, grab him and shake him and scream at him until he admitted that he loved me too. Instead, I reached for the tequila and took a swig straight out of the bottle. Then another one. It kept me occupied until Eric stepped up to the mic and started his set.

By the time he finished, I'd collected myself and was ready to try again. Eric took one look at me and headed in the other direction. He went straight to the bar, where he was immediately surrounded by people. I watched apprehensively. He didn't like being crowded. In fact, he'd developed a reputation around town for telling off people who got too close or touched him without announcing themselves first. People didn't understand it, but they loved it anyway because it was such a rock-star way to act. No one knew the ugly reasons for it -- not even me, not entirely -- and Eric didn't seem inclined to change that.

He turned to put his back against the bar. He smiled and talked to people and seemed perfectly relaxed, which made his admirers happy. But I could see his tension in the way he held his shoulders, and I hoped he'd be able to get away before he started panicking. Our eyes met through the forest of people. For one searing second I saw through his armor into the black hole inside him, and it broke my heart.

How I got through the set with Naked Cello that night, I'll never know. It seemed to take forever. All I could think of was Eric, and the things I wanted to say to him. I tried not to think of the things I wanted to do with him, because I didn't want an entire bar full of people to see how that affected me. So I thought about the hopelessness in his eyes, and how I could take it away and make him smile, really genuinely smile, again.

I tried to keep sight of him while I played, but he wasn't having that. He wormed his way out of the crowd at the bar only a few minutes into the set and disappeared into the back somewhere. After we were done, I told Janey that she and Mike should go on home without me, then set off in search of Eric before she could say anything.

He wasn't anywhere to be found. After I'd searched the whole place twice, it finally occurred to me that he'd probably gone up to his apartment over the bar. I climbed the narrow staircase at the back of the storage room and knocked on the door. No answer. I knocked harder.

"Eric!" I called. "You might as well let me in, 'cause I'm not leaving."

A few seconds later the door opened. Eric stood aside and let me in.

"I figured you'd be up eventually. Say whatever it is you're so hot to say and leave me alone."

I stared hard at him. "You look terrible." He did, too. He was too thin and paler than ever, and his eyes looked bruised from lack of sleep.

His smile was brief and humorless. "That what you wanted to say? Because I already knew that."

"You know that's not it. You haven't been taking care of yourself, though, have you?"

"Maybe not. Can't see that it's any of your business."

I counted to ten in my head. He was trying to piss me off, and I was determined not to let him.

"No, I don't guess it is."

He raised an eyebrow at me. "You done?"

"No." I took a deep breath and forged ahead. "Listen, I know I haven't been around lately. And I know I've kind of been…avoiding you. That was wrong, and I'm sorry. But it was just…" I fumbled for the right words. Eric leaned against the wall and watched me without expression. "It hurt that we were so distant, and I couldn't handle it, you know? I couldn't handle barely speaking to each other when I want more than that."

He shook his head. "I don't want to hear this. I think you should leave now."

"No. Not until you listen to me."

"Listen to what?" He pushed away from the wall and started pacing like a tiger in a cage. "What are you trying to say exactly, huh? That you wanted some sort of relationship with me? You're fucking crazy if you think that can ever happen, Ben. Why in hell would you want to be with someone you can't even touch? You could have anybody you wanted, why does it have to be me? Go find someone normal and just leave me the fuck alone!"

"I don't want anyone else, Eric. I want you. Sure, you have problems, but we can work them out. I want to try."

He stalked up to me with his eyes blazing. "Get this through your head, Pollyanna," he snarled. "You can't have me. Nobody can. I'm fucking damaged goods. Take off your goddamn rose-colored glasses and try to see how things really are for a change."

That was it. I snapped.

"Fuck you!" I screamed. "You're the one who can't see how things really are! How could you think that no one could ever love you again? *I* love you, you fucking idiot!"

Eric's back hit the wall and I realized I'd been backing him up. I stopped and stood there shaking. His eyes were huge and his face was gray.

"No," he said in a small, quiet voice. "You can't love me. You can't."

He looked small and lost and alone, and my anger drained away. "I do. I've been in love with you right from the first. Only I was too scared to tell you."

He stared at me with panic in his eyes. "Ben, please, please, find someone else. Please."

"Why? Why should I settle for someone else? I love you, Eric. And I think you love me too. If you don't, I'll go away and not bother you again. But I believe you do. So tell me the truth: do you love me, or not?"

A long, silent moment went by. Finally he dropped his gaze to the floor and shook his head. "No," he whispered.

He was obviously lying, though I couldn't figure out why. I laid my hands on his shoulders, careful not to grab too hard and set off his self-defense reflex. "You're lying. Tell me the truth."

He closed his eyes and leaned back against the wall. "I, I don't love you, I don't…"

"Look at me, Eric! Look at me and tell me the fucking truth!" My fingers dug into his arms. He twisted loose so fast I hardly knew what was happening and pushed me away. His eyes locked onto mine, and his agony nearly ripped me open.

"Okay!" he shouted. "Yes! Yes, I fucking love you! Does that make you happy? Fuck!"

He clenched his fists, and for a second I was sure he was going to bust either the wall or my face. Then his fingers relaxed, and he buried his face in his hands and slid down the wall to sit on the floor. I dropped down beside him and pried his hands away so I could see his eyes. His gaze was dull and dead.

"Yes. It does make me happy." I raised a hand to caress his cheek. He couldn't hide the raw need in his eyes when I touched him.

"You don't understand what this means." His voice was flat with despair.

"Tell me. I want to understand why you're so afraid."

He stared solemnly into my eyes. "Because, everyone I've ever loved is dead. Everyone. For a little while, with Jason, I thought maybe I could have a normal life, that I could...I could love someone, and he could love me. But Jason died. And, I can't live with myself if anything happens to you. I was so fucking stupid to think we could be together, but it felt so good to be with you, Ben, it was so easy. But when you touched me...fuck, I wanted you to, I did! I guess I needed to be reminded what I am. I'm poison, Ben."

It hurt so bad to hear him say those things about himself, and to know he really believed them. I cupped his face in my hands and leaned close. "You're not poison. I don't know what's happened to you to make you think that about yourself. But it's not true. You don't need to keep hiding, Eric. You need someone to help you. Let me help you, please."

The war going on inside him was painful to watch, but I kept still and didn't say anything else. I couldn't force him to let me in. He had to do it himself. Finally he reached up and slid his hands through my hair, urging me closer. I slipped one arm around his waist, cupped the back of his head with my other hand, and laid a gentle kiss to his mouth. His lips trembled against mine.

"I-I lied. About how Jason died, I mean. I lied to you."

"It's okay," I whispered. "I'm here, and I'm not leaving you. Not ever. Tell me."

He drew a deep, trembling breath. "He was with me when...when those men attacked me. It was dark, and we didn't see them. They took us by surprise. One of them had a gun. He told us he'd kill us if we didn't do what they said. They, they made Jason...they made him...shit. Shit! They fucking raped him, and I couldn't stop it. I kept looking for an opening, to get that fucking gun away, but I never got it. And...and when they were finished with him, they cut his throat. God, he fucking bled to death while I watched, and I couldn't help him, they wouldn't let me help him! I fought them, but I couldn't take all of them. They beat me until I couldn't fight anymore, then they, they ra -- raped me too. And they cut me open and left me to die. I wanted to die. But I woke up two weeks later in the hospital, and I was still alive, and Jason was dead, and it was all my fault. I, I don't even know where he's buried. Fuck, Ben..."

The tears finally came then, tears that had been held back for far too long. He curled up and sobbed against my chest, clinging to me like I was the last sane thing in the world. I pulled him into my lap and held him, stroking his back and rocking him like a child. I couldn't even speak. I felt cold and numb with shock at the things he'd had to endure.

Eventually his sobs became sniffles, his shivering slowed and stopped, and he lay still and quiet in my arms. I combed my fingers through his hair and kissed his cheek. He wound an arm around my neck.

"Thank you," he whispered.

I smiled. "You're welcome."

"Stay with me tonight?" He raised his head and gazed pleadingly at me.

"Of course I'll stay," I told him. He smiled at me and it warmed me all over.

We brushed our teeth, sharing Eric's toothbrush, then stripped down to our underwear and climbed into bed. There wasn't even a thought of sex. Even if he'd been ready for it, which he wasn't, we were both way too exhausted. But when he kissed me and cuddled against me, with his head on my chest and his arm over my stomach, I didn't need anything else.

"I love you, Ben," he murmured as his eyes drifted closed.

"I love you too," I answered around the sudden lump in my throat.

He sighed and was instantly asleep. I tried to stay awake a little longer, wanting to savor the feel of his heart beating against me, but it was no use. My eyes closed and sleep sucked me under.

Chapter Nine

I stood in the shadow of a huge oak tree, watching as Eric climbed the steps onto the wide front porch of the house. At the top of the steps he turned and called to me. I tried to answer and couldn't, so I swallowed my fear and started across the stretch of neatly tended grass between the woods and the mansion.

In the blink of an eye, I was standing on the porch and Eric was gone. The front door hung open; inside it looked pitch black. I tried to call Eric's name, but couldn't make a sound. Somehow, I knew he'd gone inside, and that I had to follow. I stepped through the door.

Enough moonlight peeked through the windows to light my way. I was standing in an elegant parlor, decorated with expensive furniture and priceless paintings. Eric stood in the doorway on the other side of the room. He was naked, and his skin glowed with a light that seemed to come from inside him. He smiled at me, turned, and disappeared into the darkness beyond the door. I followed him.

I ran through room after room, chasing glimpses of Eric deeper into the house. As I went, the rooms grew progressively smaller, darker, and dirtier. And as the filth and ugliness of the house increased, Eric's beauty grew, until the sight of him shining in the dark seared my vision and all I could see was him. Stumbling blindly on through the blackness, I followed his light wherever it led.

Finally, I emerged onto a tiny back porch with rotten floors, where Eric stood waiting for me. I made my way across the sagging floor to him. Things I didn't want to see skittered around my feet as I walked. Eric's bare skin radiated white light all around, and his eyes glowed a soft sapphire. His beauty brought tears to my eyes.

"Ben," he said, his voice muffled and wavery as if he was speaking underwater. "Be with me now, Ben."

He opened his arms and I went to him. As we embraced, I knew that I would die, but all I felt was a happiness deeper than any I'd ever known. And when we kissed and I felt my life draining away, I sank into death with a sense of peace.

The first thing I saw when I opened my eyes was Eric's face, glowing with light. For a second dream blended with reality and I thought I was dead. Then I realized that I was in Eric's bed, and the morning sun was shining in and illuminating his face. He was lying beside me, propped up on one elbow, watching me. He traced a fingertip down my cheek and it came away sparkling with wetness.

"You were crying in your sleep."

"Had a bad dream. Well, not exactly bad, just…weird." I couldn't really explain how I'd felt in my dream, so I didn't try. Me dreaming about dying in his arms would most likely upset him, even though I'd found it strangely comforting.

He smiled at me. "So, what now?"

I yawned and stretched and ended up with my head in his lap. He raked his fingers through my hair and I grinned up at him. "I'd sure like for you to move back in with me. But it's up to you. You might want to have some space to yourself, for a while anyhow."

He chewed his bottom lip thoughtfully. That was so distracting, I had to sit up and chew on it myself for a while. He laughed when I nabbed his lip between my teeth and sucked on it like a piece of candy.

"Stop distracting me!" he said when we finally stopped kissing several minutes later.

"You started it," I pointed out. "Do you even know how fucking sexy it is when you bite your lip like that? It drives me crazy."

He laughed and leaned his forehead against mine. "I'm so happy right now. I never thought I could be happy again." He pulled away and stared hard at me. "It scares me."

I took his hand and squeezed it. "What are you scared of?"

"I'm scared of how good I feel. I keep thinking I'll wake up and it'll all be a dream. This feels too good to be real."

I pulled him to me and gave him a long, thorough kiss. "It's real, Eric. I love you."

He cradled my face in his hands, very gently, as if he thought I might break. "I want you so much." He flicked his tongue over my lips. "I want...I want you to touch me."

The thought of that made all the blood in my brain rush straight to my cock. "What?"

He smiled. "Touch me. I think maybe it'll be okay now. Here…"

He took my hand and laid it on the curve of his hip. I about stopped breathing when he guided my hand slowly down the outside of his thigh, around to the inside, and back up again. He let go and I kept moving until the tips of my fingers were nearly touching his groin. I stopped and stared hard into his eyes. He stared back with enough heat to burn down the building.

"Please, Ben." His voice was a hoarse whisper and his entire body begged me to do it. So I slid my hand up that last little bit and brushed my palm against the hardness straining the fabric of his underwear.

A tremor ran through him and he gasped out loud. "Oh, oh fuck!"

"You okay?" I couldn't help being worried, in spite of the lust in his eyes.

"Yes," he moaned. "God, that feels so fucking good. C'mere."

He grabbed me by the hair and pulled me down on top of him. I tried to say that maybe that wasn't such a good idea. But his tongue in my mouth and his hands shoving inside my underwear made me forget all about protesting. I managed to keep myself from ripping off the thin cotton that still covered him, but he sure didn't make it easy. If this was a taste of what sex with him would be like, I was in for a wild ride. He was fierce and aggressive, marking me with his teeth and his short fingernails.

I don't know what would've happened if we'd tried to take it slow. Maybe we could've made love then. Probably not. But that's not what happened. My self-control was just about gone when he wrapped his legs around my waist, pushing our cocks together through the fabric still separating us. I groaned into his mouth and couldn't help thrusting against him.

For a second everything was fine. He arched his back and tightened his legs around me. Then all of a sudden his body stiffened, his eyes went wide, and he pushed frantically on my chest.

"Off, get off," he squeaked. I rolled off of him. He sat up and huddled against the headboard, shaking all over and gasping for breath.

"Eric? Jesus, are you all right?" I reached a hand out to him, then thought better of it. He didn't look like he wanted to be touched right then.

For a minute he didn't answer me. Finally he looked up at me and nodded. "Yeah, I'm okay now. Christ, Ben, I'm so sorry. I really thought it was okay this time. Fuck."

He drew his knees up and rested his head against them. I crawled over to him, wrapped my arms around him, and pulled him close.

"It'll be all right. We'll just have to take this slower, that's all."

"I don't want to go slow." His voice was muffled against my neck. "I want you now, right now. I don't want to wait."

I smiled and kissed his hair. "Me too. But you know I'm right. Hell, after what you've been through it's no wonder you have panic attacks. Anyone would."

He raised his head to look at me. "You think so?"

I stared at him with my mouth hanging open. "You're kidding, right? Come on, there's not one person in this world who could live through what you did and not have huge problems after."

"My dad said I deserved everything that's happened to me. He said I brought it all on myself by being such a bad person. He said it was my fault Jason died." He fell silent, staring at the wall. His face was white. I frowned in disbelief.

"Eric, I don't know why your father would say something like that, but he's wrong. You are not a bad person, and you sure as hell didn't deserve what happened to you. And it was not your fault that Jason died."

He gave me a sad little smile. "How do you know? Maybe it was."

"I don't see how. He was murdered, Eric. That wasn't your doing."

He shook his head. "I don't know, Ben. Something's wrong with me. If I was normal, the people I love wouldn't keep ending up dead."

"Stop that." I laid my hand on his cheek and kissed the end of his nose. "Jason's death was not your fault. His rape was not your fault. The things those bastards did to you were not your fault either. You're a good person, Eric, and there's nothing wrong with you that a good therapist can't help you fix. You're just like everyone else. Only sexier."

He looked startled for a second, then busted out laughing. "I swear, only you could crack me up like that in the middle of a dead-serious conversation."

I grinned at him. "It was either that or start yelling at your dad, and that would be kind of pointless since he isn't here and I wouldn't know him from Adam's house cat anyhow."

He laughed, then launched himself into my arms. We tumbled back onto the mattress, with Eric on top this time.

"I don't want to talk about my father. I don't want to think about him, I don't want to remember he even exists. I just want to enjoy this before it ends."

"It doesn't have to end. We love each other, Eric. This is the real thing and we can make it last."

He traced my lips with his thumb, making my pulse race. "How? You're gonna get tired of being stuck with someone who freaks out every time you do anything more than kiss him."

"Listen to me. I love you. That means I'm not just looking for a good time, and I'm not going to bail on you when things get tough. I'm in this for the long haul, whatever that might mean. Sex is great, but it's not all there is. I'll wait for you as long as you need me to."

He gazed down at me with hope and fear in his eyes. "Don't die, Ben," he said, so softly I could barely hear him.

His words, coming on the heels of my dream, sent a chill up my spine. *Everyone I've ever loved is dead,* he'd said the night before. I shook off my unease and concentrated on Eric. I didn't know what to say. There was really no way to ease his mind without promising I'd never die, and who can promise that? He let me pull him against me and rested his head on my chest. We lay like that for a long time.

Chapter Ten

I could've stayed there in his arms forever. But the world keeps turning, even when you fall in love, and both of us had other obligations. Eric was earning extra money helping out around the bar during the day, and I had to be at Marco's for the dinner shift in a few hours. Funny how they don't pay you if you don't show up.

After a while, I made myself get up and get dressed. Eric pulled on a pair of jeans and stood watching me silently. When I was ready to leave, he pressed his body against mine and kissed me like we had the rest of our lives to do nothing but that.

"I don't want you to go," he said when we finally pulled apart.

"Me neither." I ran my fingers down his bare back and smiled at the way his eyes went unfocused. "But I have to. I've got to go get some groceries, and I have to be at Marco's in, let's see..." I glanced at the clock on his shelf. "Four hours. And Tamara'll be expecting you downstairs before long."

"Yeah. Hey, will you come back after you get off work?"

"Of course I'll be here."

He slid both hands through my hair and rubbed his cheek against mine. "Love you," he whispered in my ear.

I tightened my arms around him and we kissed again. "Love you too."

It was damn hard to let him go, but I did it. He wrapped both arms around himself and bit his lip. His fear was obvious, but he didn't try to stop me.

"Don't worry." I backed out the door. "This is real, and I'm not ever letting you go. You'll see."

He smiled, but it didn't touch his eyes. "Go on."

"You gonna be okay?"

He nodded. "Yeah. Think I'll go for a run before work."

"Good idea. All right, see you later. 'Bye."

"'Bye."

How I managed to shut the door and walk down the stairs with him standing there looking so goddamn vulnerable, I'll never know. I walked home in a daze and went through the motions of grocery shopping without paying much attention to what I was doing. It made me laugh when I realized I'd bought twelve boxes of microwave popcorn. Thinking of the way Eric liked to play with my hair when we kissed had distracted me to no end.

I put away the groceries, then went to shower and change clothes. Mental pictures of Eric distracted me again in the shower, making me wish he was there with me. Not because I was dying to see him wet and naked, which I was, but because I missed him. It felt like we'd been apart for days instead of hours. Maybe his fear had rubbed off on me, but whatever the reason, it scared me a little to be away from him. Nothing would feel quite right until we were together again.

I actually went to work a little early, just to get away from my own overactive imagination. Janey was just finishing up on the lunch shift when I got there.

"Hi, Ben. What are you doing here already? You're not on for another half hour."

"I know. I just had to get out. My brain wouldn't turn off."

She laughed. "So what's got you all revved up? Would it have anything to do with the fact that you never came home last night?"

"How'd you know that?"

"I'm psychic."

"Aren't."

"Okay, fine. I came over and knocked on your door for probably five solid minutes this morning, and you never answered. So I figured you'd stayed at Eric's."

I grinned at her. "Yeah, I did."

"And?" She crossed her arms and raised her eyebrows at me.

"And what?"

"God, you're evil." She grabbed my arm and pulled me into the break room. "How'd it go? Did you tell him? What'd he say? C'mon, spill it."

I pulled her into an impulsive hug. "You're the best, Janey, you know that?"

She giggled. "Yes. Now are you gonna tell me what happened or not?"

"I told him I love him. And it was hard for him to accept at first, and even harder for him to admit he felt the same way. But he did, and I think we're gonna be okay."

She pulled back and smiled up at me. "I'm happy for you."

"Just me?"

She sighed. "I'm sorry, but I just don't trust him. He sets off my alarms. I don't know why, he just does. I hope everything works out for you two, really. You deserve to be happy. But I can't lie and say I like him when I don't."

I couldn't hide my disappointment. "I don't want you to lie. But I wish you didn't feel this way. It's hard knowing my best friend hates the man I'm in love with."

"I don't hate him."

"You don't like him either."

"I'd change how I feel if I could."

"I know."

There really wasn't anything else to say. Janey told me she and Mike would be at The Alley Kat later on, hugged me goodbye and headed for home. I got my assignment and went to work.

It was slow for a Saturday, and the time seemed to crawl by. My mind kept wandering to Eric. I wondered what he was doing right then, and if he was thinking of me, and whether he missed me as much as I missed him.

"Excuse me?"

I came back to earth and saw that I was pouring iced tea into an old lady's coffee cup. "Oh, sorry. I'll get you some fresh coffee."

"No, don't bother," the woman said with a smile. "I was just getting ready to leave." She glanced down at the newspaper she'd been reading and shook her head. "Terrible thing about those boys, isn't it?"

"What do you mean?"

"You haven't heard? The police arrested a man yesterday on drug charges, and when they searched his house they found several bodies of young men in his basement."

"Seriously? Wow, that's awful. Does it say the guy's name?"

She glanced back at the paper. "Yes, his name's Adam Richardson. Do you know him?"

I shook my head. "Nope. Thank God. So what did he do to them?"

"He'd tortured and killed them and kept their bodies in a big walk-in freezer. Terrible thing. It's frightening to think of such a monster living right here in our midst, isn't it?"

"It sure is." It gave me the crawls to think of someone like that walking around Asheville. Maybe he'd even been in here before. Maybe I'd served him pizza and beer. The thought made me feel cold inside. "Wonder how come there wasn't anything on the news before about these guys going missing?"

"Apparently there haven't been any reports of young men missing from Asheville. Of course not all of the victims have been identified yet, so some of them could be missing from other areas of the country. But the police believe they may have been homeless and without any family, at least not in this area. They said he must have researched his victims and watched them for a little while before he struck. They think he lured them to his home by promising them food and shelter. And he…" She stopped suddenly and blushed crimson, then leaned toward me and continued in a whisper. "He did things to them. You know."

I got the point. The guy wasn't just a murderer, he was a sexual predator as well. Nice. "I'm glad they caught him," I said with feeling.

"Me too, dear." She gave me a sweet smile as she stood up and hoisted her purse onto her shoulder. "Goodnight, and do be careful out there. You just never know about people."

"I'll be careful and you be careful too. 'Night." She waved at me and headed for the door.

I started cleaning off the table. The newspaper was still opened to the article she'd been reading and I picked it up to have a look. When I saw the picture, my head started swimming and I had to sit down.

Adam Richardson was the man Eric had fought with the night we met.

Chapter Eleven

I thought about bringing the paper with me, but in the end I decided not to. The thing felt dirty. My imagination, of course, but I still didn't think I could stand to walk even a few blocks with that freak's picture in my hand. There would probably be a paper at The Alley Kat if I just had to have one.

I was completely torn about whether or not to tell Eric. He deserved to know, but there was no way he was going to take the news well. By the time I got to The Alley Kat, though, I'd decided that I had to tell him. He'd find out one way or another anyhow, and I figured it would be better if he heard it from me.

Eric had finished his set for the night and was behind the bar helping Malcolm when I got there. The place was packed and I had to elbow my way through the crowd to get up to the bar. Malcolm caught my eye, and I motioned him over.

"Hi Ben!" he shouted over the noise of the crowd and the machine-gun punk screaming from the speakers. "You took my advice, huh?"

"Yeah," I shouted back, "but how'd you know? Eric tell you?"

"Nope. But he's a different man today. Wasn't hard to figure out why."

I grinned. "You're a pretty smart dude for a bartender, you know?"

"I know. What'll you have?"

"Nothing right now, I just need to borrow Eric for a while."

"Okay, I can handle this mob for few minutes. Just make it a quickie, huh?"

"That's not it, smartass. I found out something that he needs to know, and I thought it would be easier for him to hear it from me than from the news."

Malcolm's face grew very serious. He leaned over the bar towards me. "You saw the story about that guy, huh?"

I nodded. "Yeah. Does Eric know?"

"Don't think so. You know we don't turn the TV on much in here, and I stuck the paper under the bar. I figured he'd take it better if you were with him when he heard."

"Thanks, man."

"No problem." He turned and called to Eric, who was swamped at the other side of the bar and hadn't spotted me yet. "Eric! Ben's here!"

Eric turned, and his eyes lit up when he saw me. He mouthed "hi" to me, then turned back to the girl he'd been helping. He handed her a bottle of beer and took the five she gave him to the register. I tried not to laugh when he handed her back her change and she trailed her fingers up his arm. He ignored her and turned toward me with a big smile on his face.

Couldn't blame her for giving it a try. His snug jeans and T-shirt showed off his athlete's body, his eyes glittered in the low light, and his lips begged to be kissed. I wondered if he noticed that practically everyone at the bar was watching him.

"Ben!" He leaned over the bar, grabbed my hair in both hands and kissed me with great enthusiasm. I forgot about everything else and kissed him back.

"I missed you," he said when we came up for air.

I stroked his cheek and smiled at him. "Me too."

"How was Marco's?"

"Slow. I think everybody's here tonight instead."

He laughed. "Yeah, I think you're right. The place has been hopping all night."

He looked so happy. I'd never seen him look quite like that, not even when he sang. It seemed like he'd gotten over the fear and uncertainty he'd felt that morning, and I hated the thought of telling him about what could've happened to him. For a minute I considered not telling him after all. But in a town like Asheville, that sort of crime is almost unheard of, and it would be in the news a lot in the coming weeks. He'd find out, and he'd wonder why I hadn't told him.

"Ben? What's wrong?"

His eyes were wary. I took his hand, kissed his palm, and laid it against my cheek. "I need to tell you something. Malcolm said I could borrow you for a few minutes."

He stiffened and pulled his hand away. "What?"

It killed me to see the hurt in his face, and see him trying so hard to hide it. I stood, walked around behind the bar, pulled him to me and kissed him until I felt the tension leave his body.

"Not what you're evidently thinking. I love you. Now come on, let's talk."

He gave me a sheepish grin. "Sorry. I just can't get my head around this, you know?"

He told Malcolm that we were going to the storeroom where it was quieter to talk, and we set off hand in hand. We sat down at the little table in the corner and he looked at me expectantly.

"Okay. So what's this all about? You look awfully serious."

"Yeah." Now that we were here, I didn't know how to begin. I sat with his hand firmly clutched in mine and tried to think how to say it.

"Come on, Ben, you're making me nervous here," he said. "Just spit it out."

"Okay. Yeah. Okay, you remember that guy you were fighting with the night we met?"

He made a face. "Sure do. Bastard. He was trying to get me to go home with him."

My stomach turned over at the thought of what could've happened if he'd gone with the guy. "Well, it's a good thing you didn't. He was arrested yesterday. It was a drug trafficking charge, but they found several bodies of young men in his basement. They'd been tortured and sexually abused."

All the color drained from his face. "Oh shit," he said weakly.

I reached out and cupped his cheek in my hand. "You all right?"

He glanced up at me and his eyes were huge. "He said he'd take me to his place up in the mountains. Said it was really remote and secluded, and he only took special people there. Jesus."

I frowned. "Wait a minute, the paper said his house was in the city. It didn't say anything about another property."

He managed a weak smile. "Inflating his assets. He probably would've said anything."

"Hm. Probably. It'd be a good idea if you told the police anyhow, though. There might be more bodies if he's got another place they don't know about."

He shook his head. "No, I'm sure he was just lying. There's no reason for me to go to the cops."

"I really think you should. What if he's got some guy up there that's still alive?"

For a second doubt showed in his face. Then it was gone behind a wall of stubbornness that would eventually become very familiar to me. "No. He was just making it up so I'd go with him."

"Eric, I really think…"

"No!" he interrupted angrily. "I'm not going to the fucking cops!"

I stared at him with my mouth open. He stared at the table.

"It's not important, that's all," he mumbled. "No reason to bother the police."

We sat in silence for a moment. Finally I had to ask. "Why don't you want to go to the cops, Eric?"

"I told you."

"No, you didn't. What's the real reason?"

He wouldn't look at me. "I haven't done anything wrong."

"Then why won't you go talk to them?"

"Yeah, Eric. Why? What are you hiding?"

Janey's voice made us both jump. I frowned at her. "Janey! What the hell are you doing?"

"Malcolm sent me to get some more Margarita salt." She walked toward us with her arms crossed and sparks shooting from her eyes. "I was helping him out while you guys were busy talking. Guess I came along at just the right time."

"What's that supposed to mean?"

"It means," she answered, "that you, Ben, are too trusting for your own good. Can't you see that he's playing you? For God's sake, if someone's that scared of the cops there must be a reason for it."

Eric stood up and glared at her. "You stay out of this."

Janey glared right back at him. "I will not!"

I gritted my teeth and tried not to lose my temper completely. "Whatever his reasons are, he'll tell me when he's ready. I trust him."

"That's your biggest problem, Ben," she said. "You trust everybody."

"Not everybody, but I love Eric. And if you love someone, you should trust them; otherwise it doesn't mean a damn thing."

"Goddamnit, Ben!" she shouted. "You have no idea who the hell he is or what he's done! Wake the fuck up!"

Eric took a step toward her. His fists were clenched tight. "You don't know a fucking thing!" he shouted. "What, you just assume that I'm wanted or something just because I don't trust the cops? Believe me, if you'd seen the things I have, you wouldn't trust them either."

Janey stalked up to him. "Oh, were the bad old cops mean to poor little Eric? Whatever you got, asshole, you probably deserved it."

Eric's eyes darkened. His tough-guy mask snapped into place faster than you could blink, but I'd seen the anguish that flooded his face for a split second. He still half-believed that his attack and Jason's death were his own fault. That was it. Janey had crossed a line I couldn't let her cross, even if she didn't realize what she'd done. I stepped between her and Eric.

"Get out," I told her. "Get the fuck out and don't talk to either of us again until you can treat Eric like a human being."

She gaped at me. "You don't mean that."

"The hell I don't. This isn't some little fling, Janey. Eric and I love each other, and you're going to have to accept that."

She bit her lip. "He's dangerous, Ben, why can't you see that?"

"Don't talk about me like I'm not here," Eric said between clenched teeth. "I'd never hurt him, not ever. Can't say the same for you."

I laid a hand on his arm; he fell silent and backed up a pace.

"He's not dangerous, Janey."

"I'm your best friend, Ben. He's a stranger, probably even a criminal. I can't stand by and watch you fuck up this bad."

"Then we have nothing else to say to each other."

Tears welled in her eyes. She started to say something, stopped, then turned and walked out of the room. I didn't try to stop her.

I turned to Eric. His eyes were snapping and he looked like he wanted to run after Janey and break her in half. But, when he saw my face, his expression softened. He came to me and took me in his arms.

"I'm so sorry," he whispered, and that was all it took. I buried my face in the curve of his neck and sobbed.

Whether Malcolm ever got his Margarita salt or not, I have no idea. If he came after it himself, I never heard him. When I couldn't cry any more, Eric led me upstairs and helped me through the business of getting ready for bed. He tucked me under the covers, climbed in beside me and spooned against my back. He stroked my hair and sang softly to me until exhaustion finally overcame the pain of losing my best friend, maybe for good. Sleep eventually took me, to the whispered sound of an old lullaby and the warmth of Eric's body against mine.

Chapter Twelve

The next few days were pretty rough. I switched shifts with another waiter at Marco's so I wouldn't have to be around Janey. It was just too painful to see her. The fact that I was right and she was wrong didn't make it any easier. I loved her, and I missed her horribly. There were lots of times that I picked up the phone to call her, then put it down again, still stinging from the things she'd said.

During those days, Eric gave me a strength I didn't have on my own. He listened to me alternately curse Janey's existence and wax nostalgic about all the good times we'd had. He never once put Janey down, or told me I was better off without her, even though he had plenty of reasons to. Besides, I did enough of that myself for both of us. He simply let me talk and seemed to sense that's what I needed to do.

It didn't surprise me at all when Eric tried to take the blame for what had happened, but it still hurt to see him trying to put another undeserved burden on himself. I told him, truthfully enough, that it wasn't his fault; it was Janey's fault for being so bullheaded. His protests stopped when I kissed him, and he didn't say anything else about it.

Most days when I wasn't working, I stayed with Eric. Most nights too. Sometimes we'd stay at my place, mostly because he thought it was a waste of rent money if I wasn't ever there. A fair point, but I just didn't like being there anymore. It didn't feel like home without Janey coming over all the time.

"Maybe I should just move in with you," I speculated one afternoon. We were lying on my floor listening to Rufus Wainwright and talking about our living arrangements. "My lease is up next month, so I either have to renew or move out."

"Do you think we can both live in that small a space?"

"Why not? It's not like either one of us has lots of stuff or anything. You got room for my CD collection, that's all I need."

He laughed and rolled onto his side. "Yeah, there's room. I need something to fill up the shelves."

I grinned at him. "Then I guess you've got yourself a roommate."

"Great!" He propped himself up on one elbow and leaned over me, his lips curving into a seductive smile. "You're such a piece, you know that?" He leaned down and brushed his mouth against mine.

"Yeah, sure. I'm the one everybody in town's mooning over, right?" I kissed the corner of his mouth and felt him smile.

"You don't have a clue how gorgeous you are, do you?" He pulled back and stared down into my eyes. It was a good thing I was already lying down, because the way he looked at me made my legs feel all rubbery. "Let me tell you what, I've lost track of how many girls have asked me if you're single."

"No hot guys?" I pretended to pout.

He grinned. "Plenty of those too."

"Well, I hope you sent 'em packing."

"Some of them were already packing."

"Smartass."

"Yep."

"C'mere."

I pulled him down to me and we kissed again. His mouth was soft and warm, and he tasted so sweet. I wanted to drown in him.

"God, Ben," he whispered, "I want you so bad." He trailed tiny kisses over my jaw and down my throat, making me shake inside.

"Shit, I want you too." I buried my hands in his hair as he worked his way back up to my mouth.

Our kisses grew more and more heated, until we were eating at each other like it was our last moment on earth. My hands kept drifting down his back, and I kept making myself stop before I lost all control and ripped his clothes off. I had to bite my lip to keep from crying out when he yanked my T-shirt up and bent to suck at my nipple.

"Eric...oh, oh God...what...I mean, are you...oh..." I couldn't say what I wanted to say, but he understood me anyway.

"Fine, I'm fine," he mumbled against my chest. His lips traced down my ribs and over my belly, and I gasped when he lifted my hips and dipped his tongue just under the waistband of my jeans.

"B-but…"

He sat up almost faster than I could see and straddled my hips. His mouth covered mine again before I realized what was happening. "I need you, Ben," he murmured as he kissed me. "I need you. Please."

He slipped a hand between my legs, massaging my groin through my jeans. I moaned and pushed up against his palm. It felt so damn good for him to touch me like that. His tongue flicked over my lips and I opened for him.

Even with pure lust burning inside me, I was worried enough about him that I managed to keep my hands out of his pants. This time, the trouble came when he unzipped my jeans and started to worm a hand inside. His fingertip brushed the head of my cock and suddenly he went still. He made a small sound in the back of his throat, then pulled away and got off of me. He drew his knees up and covered his face with his hands. I could hear his teeth chattering.

As soon as I felt like I could move again, I zipped up and sat on my knees, facing him. I touched his arm and he raised sorrowful eyes to me. "Was it another panic attack?" I asked gently.

He nodded. "I fucking hate this."

"I know." I pulled him into my arms and kissed his forehead. "Sorry. I should've stopped you, I knew it was too soon."

He shook his head against my shoulder. "I wouldn't have listened. You're so damn hot, it makes me crazy. All I can think about is sex. Do you know how long it's been since I've felt that way? And then I have to freak out every time we do anything. Shit."

"We just have to be patient, that's all."

"I don't want to be patient." He wrapped his arms around my waist and nuzzled my neck. "I just want to fuck 'til we can't get it up anymore."

I had to laugh. "Yeah, me too, but you're not ready yet. It takes a long time to recover from all the shit you've been through."

"Huh."

I lifted his chin and our eyes met. "Hey, just think how good it's gonna be when it finally happens."

He smiled. "You're amazing, you know? Most guys wouldn't put up with all this."

"Their loss." I cupped his face in my hand. "You're worth the wait, Eric. I love you."

He didn't say anything, but the love and gratitude in his eyes said it all. He lifted a hand to gently caress my cheek, then leaned in for a long, lingering kiss.

We were still at it several minutes later, when a knock on the door made us both jump.

"Better get that," he mumbled with my tongue still in his mouth.

"Mm. Don't wanna."

"What if it's important?"

"Can't think of anything more important than this."

The knock sounded again, louder this time. I sighed. "Just a sec!" I shouted.

Eric smiled, and I kissed his nose. "Be right back." I stood, opened the door, and found myself face to face with Janey. There was an awkward silence.

"Um, hi," Janey said finally. "Can I come in?"

I stood aside and she edged past me. It wasn't her usual purposeful stride at all. Eric got up off the floor and came to me, and I laced my fingers through his. Janey watched us silently.

"What is it, Janey?" I asked.

She bit her lip. "I, um, I came to apologize. To both of you. I was wrong."

I stared at her, not sure what to say. "What changed your mind?"

"Mike," she said. "I guess I've been kind of moody lately, after that fight you and I had. I yelled at him for some little thing or other last night, and we had a huge argument, and then we ended up talking for a long time. He told me straight out that I'd been wrong to say the things I did about Eric, and he thought I'd only done it because of Alan. And I had to admit that he was probably right."

Eric frowned. "Who's Alan?"

Janey and I looked at each other. "My brother," she said. "He killed himself when I was seventeen. The woman he married turned out to be using him for his money. And I know none of it would've happened if he hadn't believed everything she said without question. And I believed her too, which just made it worse. The whole business made me kind of cynical. I'm sorry, Eric. I had no right to say those things about you."

He stared at her with a strange expression on his face. He looked pale and shocked. I frowned. "Eric? You okay?"

He glanced at me, then back at Janey. "It's okay," he said. "I don't blame you for being upset. Ben's your friend; you were just protecting him. And for what it's worth, I totally understand where you're coming from."

She gave him a tentative smile. "You do?"

"Yeah. I'm kind of that way myself. My sister shot herself right in front of me when I was ten and she was fifteen. The circumstances were different, but it leaves the same sort of scars."

"God, I'm sorry." She stared at him with a new sympathy.

"Me too. It sucks that you lost your brother that way." He held out his hand to her. "Friends?"

She smiled. "Friends."

They shook hands. I watched them look at each other with understanding for the first time and felt weak with relief. When Eric stepped back, I gathered Janey into my arms and hugged her hard. She rested her head on my shoulder.

"I missed you so much," she said. She raised her face again; her eyes glittered with wetness.

"I missed you too." I thumbed the tears off her cheeks. "Nobody's given me hell for days."

She laughed. "Yeah, well. Okay. I gotta go."

"Okay." I let her go and she headed for the door. "'Bye Janey. See you later."

"'Bye," she echoed. She waved at us and was gone.

Eric's arms slid around me from behind. I leaned back against him, turned my head and kissed the angle of his jaw.

"I'm glad you guys made up."

"Me too. I really missed her, you know? She can be a pain, but we've been friends a long time and I love her."

"I know."

I turned in his arms. "I can't imagine what that must've been like. To be that young, and watch your sister die like that."

He gave me a strange look. "Ben, can I tell you something?"

"You know you can." I kissed him and he smiled, then pulled back and took off his T-shirt.

"You remember this?" He pointed at the white scar on his collarbone.

"Yeah. You said it was an accident."

"I lied. It was no accident. Sarah shot me, right before she shot herself."

I stared at him in shock. "What? She shot you?" I reached out and ran my fingers over the old scar. "Why?"

"She wanted to protect me."

"Protect you? By shooting you?"

He closed his eyes. "She was schizophrenic. The drugs helped some, but not enough, and Dad wouldn't let her go to therapy. He always thought it was a waste of time. And there were...well, other things. Things that happened, that she didn't tell anyone. Only me, and only right before she shot herself. She told me that she was afraid the same thing would happen to me, and so she had to kill me to save me from it."

"From what?"

His eyes opened again and pierced me like an iron spike. "Who knows if it was even true? I mean, she had hallucinations all the time, she never knew what was real and what wasn't. Maybe it only ever happened in her mind."

I took his face in my hands. His skin was cool to the touch. "What, Eric? What was she trying to protect you from?"

He stared at me with wide eyes. "Our father," he said finally. "She said he'd...done things to her. For years. And she, she didn't want him to do that to me. She thought nothing could hurt him, or stop him. So she tried to kill me, to keep him away from me." He laughed bitterly. "She always was a lousy shot."

I stood there, stunned into silence for a minute. "Did he ever touch you?" The thought was unbearable. But I had to know.

Eric dropped his gaze to the floor. He nodded. "Sometimes."

That hit me hard. I felt sick. A pure, perfect rage burned in my gut. Violence had never been something I understood before, but at that moment I knew what it was to want to rip someone apart and watch them bleed. I'd never met Eric's father, and I hoped I never would. If he had come through the door right then, I'd have killed him with my bare hands.

"Ben?" Eric's voice was so soft I could barely hear him. "Do you hate me now?" He was white and shaking. A single tear slipped down his cheek as I watched.

"No. God no, I could never hate you." I pulled him into my arms, hugging him against me as if I could protect him from his own past. "Eric, shit. Shit. That bastard. He had no right."

My eyes squeezed shut and I buried my face in his hair. He smelled so good, his skin was so smooth and soft under my hands. I wanted to burn him into all five senses and keep him there. I wanted to take away all the pain of his past, build a wall around him and keep anything hurtful from ever touching him again. He raised my face to his, and I kissed his beautiful mouth.

"No one should have to go through what you did. No one. He had no right to do that to you, you hear me? No right at all."

He melted into my arms, his hands clinging to my shirt in a death grip. "I know that now. It wasn't so easy when I was ten though. He said he was my father, and he could do whatever he wanted. It took me years to realize he couldn't. When I was fourteen I broke his arm, and he never tried it again. I was in lockup for six months after that, but it was worth it."

"He abuses you for years, and you get locked up for defending yourself? That's just fucking wrong."

"Yeah, well, that's how it is. His word against mine, he was bound to win."

"What about your mother? Didn't she ever notice anything? I mean with your sister too."

"My mom drowned when I was five. I can barely remember her; I just remember crying at her funeral. My dad raised us by himself after that."

I thought of my own childhood, my parents and my brother, how happy we'd all been, and how close we still were. My parents had lived in California for years, and my brother was in France, but we still talked on the phone and emailed each other all the time. It killed me to know that Eric had never had any of that. All he'd had from his family was pain.

"There's some really good therapists in town," I told him. "You should start seeing one."

He smiled against my neck. "Yeah, I'm a fucking mess, huh?"

"Actually, I think you're about the strongest person I've ever known. I'd probably be in a padded room by now."

He laughed. "You don't give yourself enough credit. Okay, so yeah, I need to go to therapy. I know that. But how am I gonna pay for it? Even if I'd been working for Tamara long enough to get insurance, which I haven't yet, I don't know if it covers stuff like that."

I thought about it for a minute. "There are programs in town that have mental health services for a reduced price. And I can help you pay for it."

He was getting ready to protest that he couldn't let me do that, but he saw the look in my eyes and stopped, then smiled.

"I love you, Ben."

"Love you too, baby."

He wrapped his arms around my neck and kissed me. I closed my eyes and concentrated on the taste of his mouth and the feel of his skin, and pushed the horrors of his past firmly to the back of my mind.

Chapter Thirteen

September came and went, and the weather started to turn cool. October brought an explosion of color with the changing leaves. Eric loved wandering the tree-lined streets in the afternoon, and we started taking long walks together, exploring the nooks and crannies of the town. It got to where he knew the place even better than I did. He finally got me to go with him sometimes on his runs. I liked it a lot, which surprised me, and pretty soon I was going with him nearly every time. He had to cut his mileage for me, but he didn't seem to mind.

Eric started seeing a terrific therapist a few days after he told me about his father. I went to some of his sessions, and I liked Dr. Spencer. She had a quiet way about her that made talking to her effortless. Eric was surprised by how easy it was to tell her about the things that had happened to him. She didn't gasp in horror, or feel sorry for him, or get angry at his dad like I'd done. It was a revelation for him to realize that his past didn't have to change how people saw him now.

I let my lease drop and moved in with Eric. We had our ups and downs, like anyone else. It wasn't all sunshine and roses. Eric was still Eric, hot temper and all, even though he laughed now way more often than he used to. We had our share of disagreements, but I wouldn't have changed a thing. I'd fallen in love with all of him, not just the fun parts, and I cherished the whole prickly, mule-headed, wonderful package.

Every day brought us a little closer, and I could feel the bond between us deepening. Eric started getting bolder, slipping his hands inside my pants when we kissed and groping my backside. The first time he stuck his hand down the front instead and ran his fingertips up my shaft, I nearly came right then. It didn't go any further than that, but he didn't get panicky either, so we decided that called for a celebration. We headed down the road to the classiest bar we knew, got plastered on tequila, and started an impromptu sing-along with Eric on piano. After the bar closed, we headed home and stayed up all night talking about the future.

That was a sort of turning point. We both knew it wouldn't be long before we could take that last step and become lovers. We were both pretty diligent about regular HIV testing already, and we were both clean, so we decided to toss out the box of condoms. Eric teased that we should make it a kind of ceremony, to show our commitment to each other.

"We'll invite everybody we know." He was perched in the middle of the bed, with one foot hanging off the edge. "It can be an outdoor ceremony. We can get dressed up, and decorate the dumpster with ribbons and stuff, and have a preacher read an appropriate verse. You think Janey would play something on her fiddle? Since we'll both be busy."

"You're so full of shit." I laughed. "No way in hell are we doing that."

"Hm. The preacher's a bit much, huh?"

"Yeah. Especially since neither one of us is what you might call religious."

He pretended to think it over. "Okay, no preacher. But I'm still slapping satin ribbons all over the dumpster. And we can both wear white. You wear the dress, since you're the prettiest."

I sat up from where I'd been lying in a beam of sunlight on the floor. He seemed absolutely serious. If it wasn't for the evil gleam in his eyes, I would've thought he meant it. As it was, he didn't fool me for a second. Crawling over to the bed, I grabbed his dangling leg and pulled. He fell over onto his back.

"Hey! What're you doing?"

"I think you know. Better admit you're not really planning a throwing-away-the-condoms ceremony, or I'll do it, I swear!"

He pushed up on his elbows and gave me a look almost innocent enough to be convincing. Almost. "But I am!" He stuck out his lip. "You don't believe me."

"Damn right I don't. You gonna admit you were yanking my chain?"

He stuck his nose in the air and ignored me. I grinned. "Okay, you asked for it." I got a good grip on his ankle and ran my tongue up his instep.

He squirmed and shrieked with laughter. I'd discovered his extreme ticklishness purely by accident a couple of weeks before, and this had quickly become one of our favorite games. He hardly ever wore shoes inside, and his bare feet were easy and irresistible prey. Especially since he loved it and was constantly goading me into it.

As usual, the Licking Eric's Foot game eventually led to Sucking Eric's Fingers, which in turn led to Making Out On The Bed. We'd been doing a lot of that, even though it was getting harder and harder to stop ourselves before things got out of hand. It was mostly my own fear, not Eric's, that had kept us from going any further, because I hated the thought of him having a panic attack during sex. But this time, something felt different. I couldn't put my finger on it, but there was a change, an electric charge in the air that said anything was possible.

Eric must've felt it too. He was even fiercer than usual, which is saying a lot. When he lifted his head from where he'd been biting my neck and stared down at me, I knew this was it.

"I can't wait any longer," he said in a voice hoarse with desire. "I have to have you right now, or I'm gonna die."

He attacked my neck again before I could say a word. It took everything I had to pull him away and make him look at me.

"Are you sure?" I knew the answer already. His need was raw in his eyes.

He gave me a giddy smile. "Yeah. I'm not afraid anymore, Ben. I trust you." He grabbed two fistfuls of my hair and kissed me hard. "Let's make love, right now, c'mon."

The thought of it set a fire inside me. I stared hard into his eyes. There was no trace of the panic I'd come to recognize in our first weeks together. I reached up and cupped his face in my hands.

"We'll go slow. And you have to swear you'll tell me if you need to stop, okay?"

"Okay." He bit his lip. "You're amazing, Ben. I love you."

"I love you too. More than anything." He bent down and kissed me so tenderly that it made me ache inside.

We undressed each other as slowly as we could manage. That is to say, not very. After so long wanting and not getting, taking our time turned out to be tougher than we'd thought. I managed to get Eric's shirt and jeans off without actually tearing anything, but by then he was too frantic to even try. He balled his fists in my shirt and ripped it off, sending buttons flying, then he shoved me down onto my back. He had my jeans and underwear off in about two seconds, and I lay naked on the bed with him kneeling between my legs. He looked too hot to touch, sitting there on his knees in nothing but his black boxer-briefs.

He crawled over my body, lowered his head and licked a long, wet line up my chest. "You're so fucking sexy," he said. "I could eat you up." He bit my nipple hard and I yelped, then sighed when he licked the bite, soothing away the sting.

He nibbled his way down my abdomen, leaving a trail of bite marks behind. His hands slid down the insides of my thighs and pushed them further apart. I watched him helplessly as he dipped his head and swirled his tongue around the tip of my cock.

His mouth set off little explosions inside me. I gasped out loud and dug my fingers hard into the mattress so I wouldn't grab his head and shove my dick down his throat. That would definitely be bad.

He raised his face and stared at me with such intense hunger that it was a little scary. "You taste incredible." He wrapped one hand around my cock and flicked his tongue over the tip again, lapping up the pre-cum that dripped steadily from it. I groaned and bit my lip.

"Mm. Do you want me," he mumbled in between licks, "to suck your cock?"

I did. Just imagining it nearly undid me. But I was afraid that it would be too much too soon, and I was torn. Should've known that Eric would decide for me. He didn't wait for my answer, but opened his mouth and swallowed me whole.

"Oh, oh God!" I cried. His mouth was warm and wet and downy soft, and the muscles in his throat clenched around me in way I'd never felt before. I propped myself up on one elbow and nearly came just from the sight of his lips around my shaft.

When he tensed and pulled back, I wasn't surprised. He looked at me with such misery in his eyes that it nearly broke my heart. I held out my arms and he came to me, winding his body around mine.

"I'm sorry," he whispered. "Damn, I really thought I could. I wanted to so bad."

I stroked his hair and kissed his flushed cheek. "It's okay. I wouldn't have lasted long anyhow. Where'd you learn that trick with your throat?"

"In juvie." I must've looked as puzzled as I felt, because he laughed bitterly and explained it without me having to ask. "Juvenile lockup. I was in several times during high school. If you can suck cock really good, you don't get beat up so much." He pulled my face to his and kissed me before I could recover enough to say anything. "Let's not talk about that right now. Let's not talk at all. I'm still hard, and so are you."

I slid my hand between his legs, squeezing his thigh and letting my fingers just brush his balls through his underwear. His face softened and I felt him trembling. "I have an idea," I said, and sucked at his earlobe, "of what to do about that."

"Uh. What's that?"

I pushed him gently onto his back. "I've been wanting to suck you off for ages. Just relax."

I kissed my way down his neck and chest and over his belly. The way he shook and moaned at my touch made it damn hard to concentrate, but I forced myself to stay alert for any signs of fear or withdrawal. All I felt from him was an arousal so strong I could smell it. I curled my fingers around the waistband of his underwear and looked up into his eyes.

"Do it," he said in a raw whisper.

That was all I needed to hear. I tugged the boxers down over his hips, pulled them off and threw them on the floor. The sight of his bare body made my breath catch. I ran a hand over one firm thigh and felt him shudder.

"Jesus, you're beautiful."

He touched my cheek gently and smiled. "Love you."

"Love you too."

I bent down and planted soft kisses on each of his scars. The scar down the middle of his abdomen served as a pathway leading me to what I wanted, which was his cock, long and thick and perfect against his belly. He opened his legs. I knelt between them and took him into my mouth.

"Oh yes, God, that's good," he sighed. He raked his fingers through my hair and spread his legs wider.

It felt so great to have his cock filling my throat and sliding over my tongue. He tasted like heaven, and the way he rolled his hips against my mouth turned me liquid with need. I reached a hand out, groping blindly. He laced his fingers through mine and held on while I sucked him.

He tried to hold out, to make it last. I could feel it. But it had been a long time for him, and it wasn't long before he was on the edge. Every muscle in his body was tense and trembling with the effort of holding back. Still stroking him with one hand, I raised my head and looked into his eyes.

"Let go, baby. It's okay."

Before he could say anything, I cupped his balls in my hand and took him deep. His breath hitched, his fingers spasmed around mine, and he cried out as he came in my mouth. I swallowed the warm thick liquid as it pulsed out of him. When it stopped, I let his cock slide out of my mouth and crawled up to pull him into my arms. He melted against me and kissed me, licking his own semen off of my lips.

"God, Ben, I love you. I love you. Your mouth feels so fucking perfect."

I smiled at him and stroked the sweaty hair away from his face. "Love you too. I could suck your cock forever."

He slipped a hand down to rub his palm over my shaft, and my vision went blurry. "Let me try again," he whispered.

"Eric, I don't know if...oh God..." His hand closed around my cock, his thumb caressed the head, and I couldn't talk anymore. He chuckled low in his throat and leaned in to press his lips to mine.

"It's okay, Ben. We both want this. I've dreamed about having your cock in my mouth, and all I've had was a little taste. I want the whole thing."

I couldn't make any words come out no matter how hard I tried. But I knew he could feel how much I wanted him. He rolled me underneath him, slithered down between my legs, and slid my dick into his throat.

He was good. I'd had a glimpse of his talent before, but this was the full treatment, and it was mind-blowing. I didn't even try to hold back the sounds I was making. He lifted my hips in both hands, shoving me in deeper than I would've thought possible. The tip of my cock hit the back of his throat, his muscles grabbed me, and I felt orgasm start to wash over me.

"Oh...oh God, I'm gonna come," I gasped.

He rolled his eyes up to meet mine. His fingers dug harder into my hips, and I knew he wanted me to come in his mouth. A tiny corner of my brain feebly argued that maybe that was a bad idea, but the rest of me was too close to care. The heat in his eyes was enough to send me over the edge, and I spilled down his throat.

When the white haze cleared from my vision, he was leaning over me with a big grin on his face. I grabbed his hair in both hands and pulled him down to kiss him. His mouth opened and I could taste myself on his tongue.

"Goddamn," I said when I could talk again. "That was incredible. How the hell do you do that?"

He gave me sly smile that was cute as hell and I had to kiss him again. "I can't tell you. I'll have to show you."

"That could be interesting. Fellatio lessons; sounds like fun to me."

"We'd have to set a stiff schedule. It would be pretty hard, and it might blow up in your face."

"Oh shit," I groaned. "That's terrible."

"Hey, I can't be great at everything."

"Good to know."

He laughed, then turned serious so suddenly it made me dizzy. He laid a hand on my cheek, his thumb rubbing at the corner of my mouth. "I thought I'd never be able to make love again. I thought there'd never be anyone else. You're the best thing that's ever happened to me, Ben."

A lump rose in my throat. "I love you so much, Eric. I'm so glad we found each other."

He pulled me close, burying his face in my neck. "Love you too," he said softly.

"Sing to me?" I rested my cheek against his hair and breathed in his scent.

He laid a soft kiss on my throat. "I wrote this just now. For you."

Tears pricked my eyelids and I didn't fight them. I held him tight as his clear voice wrapped around me like a blanket.

Chapter Fourteen

The next morning, the sound of singing woke me. I lay with my eyes closed and just listened for awhile. Eric's voice floated from the bathroom, singing 'Danny Boy' in the shower.

I got out of bed, tiptoed into the bathroom, and peeked around the edge of the shower curtain. Eric stood under the water with his eyes closed, rinsing shampoo out of his hair.

"And I shall hear," he sang, "though soft you tread above me..."

I pushed the plastic curtain aside. He kept singing.

"And all my dreams will warm and sweeter be..."

I stepped carefully into the shower. He didn't seem to notice.

"If you'll not fail to tell me that you love me..."

I sidled up to him and put both arms around his waist. He smiled.

"I'll simply sleep in peace until you come to me."

He opened his eyes, pulled me to him and kissed me.

"Don't stop."

"Okay." He kissed me again, for much longer this time.

"I meant," I said when we came up for air, "don't stop singing. Although this is nice too."

"That's the end of the song." He pressed himself against me and leaned his head on my shoulder. "Besides, I've got better things to do than sing, now that you're here."

"Really?"

"Mm." He kissed his way up my throat and back to my mouth. He slipped his tongue inside and we lost ourselves for a while.

My hands wandered down his back to explore the curve of his ass. He let out a little moan that shot through me like lightning. He ran his palms down my body and wrapped a strong hand around my cock, which promptly sprang to attention. "Want this inside me," he whispered in my ear.

The thought of sticking my dick in that tight little ass sent waves of arousal rolling over me. But I didn't think he was ready for that, and I couldn't stand the thought of hurting him.

"Don't you think it's too soon? There's no rush; we've got the rest of our lives."

He stopped sucking on my earlobe and stared very seriously at me. "If there's one thing I've learned, it's that nobody ever has as long as they think."

He shoved the shower curtain aside and was gone before I could think of a single thing to say. I resisted the urge to follow him. After I finished showering, I wrapped a towel around my hips and wandered into the main room.

Eric was lying on the bed, flipping through the channels on the TV. He wore a pair of ripped, faded jeans that fit him like a second skin, and he was barefoot and shirtless. He looked so damn sexy it made my chest hurt. He glanced up at me, then back at the TV.

"Hey," he said.

"Hey. Whatcha watching?"

He shrugged. "Nothing much. Just flipping."

I nodded and sat down on the bed beside him. We watched the channels go by in silence for a few minutes. After a while, he sat up and fixed his gaze on me.

"I'm sorry. You were right. I want you inside me so bad, but it scares me too. If I react that way just from thinking about it, how much worse would I be if it really happened? That wouldn't be fair to you."

"Eric, don't wait because of me." I scooted closer and took his hand in mine. "You need to wait because that's what's right for you. You have to give yourself time."

"It's been over a year now since..." he trailed off and stared at the wall.

"Since you were raped," I finished for him.

He flinched. "Yeah."

"But you haven't been with anyone else since Jason, have you?"

He shook his head. "No. But it's been so long, Ben. A year should be enough time."

"Doesn't matter how long it's been. What matters is how you feel. Think about it, Eric. You were raped, and you almost died. Jason did die, and you were forced to watch it. You didn't get nearly the amount of therapy you needed after. All that on top of what your father did to you, and your sister, and whatever else happened in lock-up. Shit, it's amazing how well you've handled everything up 'til now, with hardly any help at all. A year isn't so long, not for all that."

He smiled wanly at me. "When did you learn so much about recovering from a...a rape?"

"Been talking to Dr. Spencer."

He stared at me. "You have?"

"Yeah. I wanted to know how to help you, that's all."

He didn't say a word. For a minute there, I thought he was really pissed. Then his eyes softened and he squeezed my hand.

"She told me that some people recover pretty fast," I said, "and others can take years, but the important thing is to give yourself that time, however long it turns out to be."

"I know. It's just...I just feel like... Hell, I don't know. I just can't shake the feeling that the other shoe's gonna drop any day and it'll all be over. That scares me more than anything."

I laid my hand on his cheek. He leaned into the caress. "We're going to be fine."

"I hope you're right."

"I am."

"I want to do everything with you. I don't want to miss a thing."

"Me neither. Don't worry, baby, we'll get there."

He ran his fingers through my wet and tangled hair. "I can still suck you off, right?"

I leaned forward and kissed him. "Hell yeah."

"Take off that towel."

* * *

A couple of hours later, we lay tangled together in a nest of rumpled sheets, naked and sweaty and sticky again. Eric curled around me with his head on my chest, clutching me to him like a security blanket. He was sound asleep. I'd propped a pillow under my head and was watching the noon news with the sound down low.

I combed my fingers through his damp hair and smiled. Ever since we'd made love for the first time the day before, he was like a kid who'd been given a million dollars and set loose in a toy store. He couldn't get enough. He'd even woken me up in the middle of the night for more. After the two times we'd just done it, I felt as worn out as he looked. My jaw ached from the unusual amount of activity, but I wouldn't have traded it for anything. I closed my eyes and let myself relive every sweet minute of it.

I woke up after several hours of deep sleep, and late afternoon shadows stretched across the room. Eric had rolled off me and was lying on his stomach, with one hand curled under his chin and the other arm hanging off the edge of the bed. He was drooling on the pillow. He looked so sweet, it made me melt inside. I slid close and kissed his cheek.

"Hm? Ben?" He stirred, yawned, and opened his eyes. "What time's it?"

I squinted at the clock. "Four. Hell, it's a good thing I didn't have to work today."

"Mm. What day is it, anyhow?"

"Thursday. And I may be off, but you've gotta play tonight. I think we're both gonna need another shower, too."

He chuckled. "That could be fun."

"You're so horny." I bit his ear and he squealed. "I like it."

"Good, because we'd have a problem if you didn't."

"Yeah?"

"Yeah. I plan on ravishing you ever chance I get."

I rolled him onto his back and kissed him. "That's a good plan."

"I thought so." He wrapped his arms around my neck and pulled me down to him.

One sixty-nine and an unusually active shower later, we finally emerged from the apartment, clean and dressed. We'd decided to head on down to the bar, since being alone with each other seemed to lead to non-stop sex. I was sore in other places besides my jaw by then. Eric wasn't ready to bottom yet, but he sure as hell didn't have any trouble topping. He'd fucked me so hard I didn't think I'd be able to walk straight for a week. My neck bore a big purplish-red mark where he'd sunk his teeth in when he came. Sex with him was even wilder than I'd thought it would be. He left me bruised and aching and more exhilarated than I'd ever felt in my life.

Eric gave me the once-over as we headed down the stairs. "Baby," he said, "you look like you just spent the whole day fucking."

"Wonder why."

He grinned. "I like that look."

"Good, because you look the same way. Only without the bite marks." I caught his hand as we reached the bottom of the steps and our fingers intertwined. "Hellcat."

He laughed as we emerged from the storeroom into the main bar. "Come on, let's get a drink. I'm buying."

Malcolm wasn't in yet, so we helped ourselves to a couple of Jack and Cokes and sat down at the bar. Mike joined us when he arrived a few minutes later.

"Hey guys," Mike said as he strolled over.

"Hey," Eric said. "Where's Janey?"

"Marco's. She switched shifts with somebody, I forget who." Mike glanced at my neck and raised his eyebrows at me. "Nice hickey."

I blushed and Eric cracked up. "Don't you have to go play or something?" I said, with as much dignity as I could manage.

Eric glanced down at his watch. "Shit, you're right." He jumped to his feet and wrapped his arms around my neck. I pulled him close and we kissed.

"Love you," I whispered in his ear.

"Love you too." He brushed a stray curl out of my eyes. "Such a piece."

I laughed. "Go on."

He grinned at me and headed for the stage.

It was a good set, one of his best. It hadn't taken me long to figure out that his songs reflected how he was feeling on any given day, and the ones he played that night brimmed with happiness. He seemed to be able to crank out new songs without even trying. Songs just flowed out of him like water.

Eric was done and the main act, a bluegrass band from Charlotte, was in the middle of their set when Janey came in. I saw her come through the door and waved at her. She hurried over to join Eric, Mike and me at the bar.

"Hi, Janey," I said.

"Hi. Look, can we go in Tamara's office? I need to tell you guys something."

Her face was pale and her gray eyes were wider than usual. I frowned. "What's wrong?"

"Not here," she said. "Come on. Eric, Mike, you need to come too."

We looked at each other as Janey started toward the office. I know we were all wondering what the hell had gotten her so worked up. We followed her silently, and Mike shut the door behind us.

"Okay, Janey," Mike said. "What's up?"

She went to Mike and wrapped both arms around his waist. He folded her in his arms and kissed the top of her head.

"He's gone," Janey said.

Eric and I looked at each other. "Who?" I asked.

"Adam Richardson," she said. "The serial killer, the one that almost got you, Eric. He's escaped."

Chapter Fifteen

"Oh, shit." I looked over at Eric. His expression radiated shock. "How? What happened?"

Mike sat down and pulled Janey onto his lap. She snuggled into his arms. "You know they were transferring him from here to the maximum security prison outside Murphy, right?"

I nodded. Needless to say, Eric and I had followed the story closely ever since it broke. We knew that the prosecution had decided to try for the death penalty. He'd been held at the medium security facility in Asheville until space opened in the overcrowded maximum security prison. He was to be transported early that morning.

"There was an accident," Janey continued. "An eighteen-wheeler ran into the van he was in. The truck driver was dead behind the wheel and they said it looked like he had a heart attack while driving. The three guards and the driver of the van all died in the accident, and Richardson escaped."

Eric licked his lips "So, they didn't catch him again? He's loose?"

"Yes. The wreck happened on a pretty deserted stretch of state highway, so by the time someone came along and called 911, he was gone. The driver that stopped didn't see him. They have no idea where he could've gone."

"Christ." Eric leaned against me and I hugged him close.

"It gets better," Janey said grimly. "The story on the news said that he must've had help to escape. He was cuffed and shackled, and the area around where the wreck happened is pretty rough and hilly. There's no way he could've gotten far on his own, and the police went over a ten mile area all around the accident with a fine-toothed comb. They even brought out tracking dogs, but didn't find a trace of him."

"They have any idea who might've helped him?" Mike asked.

Janey shook her head solemnly. "No."

"Jesus," Mike said.

I pulled Eric over to a chair and made him sit down before he passed out. He didn't even protest, which told me how shook up he really was. I knelt down in front of him and took his hands in mine.

"Eric, you have to go to the police."

He stared at me and I watched the walls go up in his eyes. "No."

"Guys," I said, without taking my eyes from Eric's face, "can you leave us alone for a few minutes?"

"Sure," Mike said. "Come on, Janey, let's go on home, huh? I'll fix you some chamomile tea."

"Okay," Janey said and I heard her walk over to us. She laid one hand on my shoulder, and the other on Eric's. "Be careful. Both of you."

I reached back and took her hand. She squeezed my fingers, then she and Mike left. I steeled myself for what I knew was going to be an extremely difficult talk.

"I know," Eric said before I could even open my mouth. "What if he's gone to his place in the woods, the police need to know he said that."

"That's true. But that wasn't what I was gonna say."

"Then what?"

"What if he comes after you, Eric? Huh? What if he's got a fixation about finishing what he starts, and he wants to finish you?"

Eric's face went blank. "I can take care of myself." His voice had a hardness I hadn't heard from him in a long time, and it scared me.

"I know you could kick his ass if it was just him. But he's got help now; maybe weapons too, who knows. And he's on the run. He won't come after you openly, he'll sneak up and take you when you're off your guard. The cops can protect you."

"No, Ben, I don't think they can. Awfully damn convenient, the way he escaped, wasn't it?"

I stared at him. "What do you mean?"

"It's no easy trick to escape from an armed police escort, wreck or no wreck. Those guards don't let up for a second. If they can hold a weapon, they've got you covered. And the vans they use are built to handle more than a normal vehicle could. It takes a hell of a blow to damage one enough to kill the people inside. So how'd it happen that all the guards died, and the prisoner wasn't even hurt? I don't believe those guards died in the crash. The van driver, maybe; but the guards? Not just one or even two, but all of them? No way. I'll give you even money they were killed after the wreck."

"But the news report said they died in the accident. They'd know that, right?"

He smiled grimly. "There are ways to make it look that way, at least at first glance. You'd be surprised."

"What are you saying?"

"I think whoever helped him escape was either a cop, or someone who was close enough to the system to know exactly what to do. I think the accident was a set-up."

"Why? And how the hell do you know so much about it anyway?"

He sighed. "Guess it's time I told you. I should've told you before, really."

"Tell me what? Eric, dammit, you're scaring me."

He stood up and started pacing. I took his place in the chair since my legs felt like rubber bands.

"If you're thinking I know by personal experience, I do. But not the way you think." He stopped, turned and looked me in the eye. "My father's a cop. He's the warden at the new maximum security prison just north of Mobile. It opened a couple of years ago, and he was promoted off the Mobile police force."

My jaw dropped open as the pieces started to click together in my mind. "So," I said, "so that's why…"

"Yeah. That's why I don't want to go to the cops. They'll put my name through their database, and they'll find out all about me. My record doesn't look good, my father made sure of that. They'll call him and tell him I'm here, if he doesn't find out by himself first. He's got access to the national database. I can't risk it, Ben. Especially now."

I stood and went over to him. "Eric, listen, I can totally understand why you wouldn't want him to know where you are. But he can't hurt you anymore. He's not the threat right now, but there is a killer out there that is. Besides, why would the cops run you through their database? You haven't done anything."

He laughed, but there was no humor in it. "Ben, I love you, but you're so naïve sometimes. They run everybody. Most people don't know that, because they don't tell you they're doing it. But they do."

"But why?"

"It's just how they do, Ben. There's no such thing as a cop without a suspicious mind. A trusting cop usually ends up being a dead cop."

"Okay, I can see that. But even if the worst happened and your dad found out you were here, what could he do? He's got no legal justification for coming after you."

"He won't sweat a little thing like legality. He'll come for me, no doubt about it."

"Why? What can he do to you now? Hell, if anything you could have him arrested, for all the things he's done to you."

He stared at me, the fear starting to show through the cracks in his armor. "You don't understand how dangerous he is."

"Then tell me. Tell me why he's so dangerous to you now, and why it's more important to keep him away than to protect yourself from a fucking serial killer."

He looked me squarely in the eye. "I think he's behind what happened to Jason and me, and I know he's the one who sent someone to kill me the night I ran. I can't risk it because if he knows where I am, he'll try again, and he won't care who he has to hurt to get me. I'll risk my life if I have to, but I'm not risking yours."

I tried to say something, but not a sound came out. I sat down and stared helplessly at Eric.

"What the fuck?" I managed finally. "Is he some kind of psycho or what? Why can't he leave you the hell alone?"

Eric sighed and rubbed his eyes. He looked so tired all of a sudden. I reached out, took his hand, and pulled him onto my lap. We wrapped our arms around each other and I felt better.

"I turned him in to the Department of Social Services a couple of months before Jason and I were attacked. He'd gotten remarried just after I got out of high school, and I saw his wife and little girl one day at the museum. They both had a few too many bruises, and the kid was afraid of her own shadow. She'd never been like that before."

"You thought he was abusing her too, didn't you?" The thought made me feel sick.

He nodded. "Yeah. So I turned him in, but when DSS went out to talk to his wife, she denied everything. There was no evidence, so there was nothing anyone could do. My arrest record didn't help any. No one believes anything I say once they find out about that."

"So, let me get this straight. You turn in your dad for, what, domestic violence, child abuse, he gets off scot-free, and he tries to kill you?"

He rested his cheek against my head and tightened his arms around me. "He didn't go to jail, but he was in the news a lot. Everybody in about three states knew about it. He barely hung onto his job as warden; lots of people wanted him out. I'm still not sure how he managed to stay in. Probably lined the right pockets. But his spotless reputation was dragged through the mud, and never did get clean again. He was plenty mad about that. And believe me, nobody holds a grudge like my father."

"So he tried to kill you. God."

"I don't have any proof, of course, but I'm sure he was behind it. He'd pretty much told me he wanted me dead."

He laid a hand on my cheek and stared into my eyes. "I used to wish I'd died that night. Now I'm glad I didn't."

I pulled him to me and kissed him. The skin of his neck was warm and soft under my hand, and his heart beat steadily against my chest. After everything I'd just heard, I felt luckier than ever to have him with me.

"Me too," I told him. "So he sent someone to try again? And that's when you left?"

"Yeah. I was having trouble sleeping, so I was dozing on the couch when the guy broke in through the bedroom window. The window squeaks, and it woke me up, so I was ready for him. When he didn't find me in bed, he came into the other room, and I jumped him. I put his own gun to his head and told him to tell me who sent him or I'd kill him. He told me it was my father. He was supposed to rough me up some, then shoot me, and leave a note calling me a filthy fag whore and saying God told him to do it."

"What? Why?"

"There'd been a rash of violence against gays in Mobile around that time. I guess Dad was hoping to pass my murder off as a gay-bashing. I'm pretty sure that's what he was going for the first time; otherwise he would've just shot me and dumped my body at sea. Or maybe he just wanted me to suffer, I don't know. He always hated me."

"Shit."

"Yeah. Anyway, I knew Dad would be waiting to hear that I was dead, and I didn't have much time. So I made the guy give me all his money, and I ran. And here I am."

I sat silent for several minutes, trying to absorb everything he'd just told me. It was a hell of a story. He about had me convinced that his father was more dangerous than Adam Richardson.

"Do you understand now?" he said, running his fingers through my hair. "Do you see why I can't let him find out where I am?"

I took his hand and kissed it. "Yeah, I can see where you're coming from. But why can't you just tell the Asheville police what all you just told me?"

He stared at me like I'd just sprouted horns or something. "You think for one second they'd believe me? No way. They'd find out about my history, or my father's version of it anyway, and they'd lock me up as a 'danger to myself and others'. I'd be a sitting duck, and so would you. No, Ben, I can't go to them. I'm sorry."

"What if you told them about how he abused you and your sister? They'd have to at least look into it, wouldn't they?"

"They wouldn't listen, even if the statute of limitations hadn't run out ages ago. My father made sure of that. He's altered all my official records to say that I have hallucinations and list 'question of schizophrenia' as the reason. It's a fucking lie, but that doesn't matter. No cop's gonna believe me when my record's so long and looks as bad as it does."

I pulled him tighter against me and buried my face in his neck. "That's not fair."

"Maybe not. But it's reality."

"Okay. So you can't go to the police in person. But listen, why don't you make it an anonymous call? That way they'd have at least some sort of lead, but they wouldn't have your name."

"They can trace the call."

"Use a pay phone. We can go anywhere in the city; there's no way the call could be traced back to you."

He still looked unsure. "I don't know, Ben."

"Okay, why don't I call, then? I'll tell them I overheard him saying he has a place in the mountains."

"But you didn't."

"So? He said it to you."

He bit his lip. "No. No, you shouldn't have to do that."

"If you won't, I will. They have to know, Eric. You know I'm right."

He was silent for a long time. Finally he sighed and pressed a hand against his eyes. "Yeah, you're right. Dammit. Okay, I'll call them. Anonymously."

I reached up and stroked his hair. "You're doing the right thing."

He nodded. "Yeah, I know. But it still scares me."

"I won't let anybody hurt you. Not that psycho killer, not your father, not anybody."

"It's not me I'm worried about. I can take care of myself." He cupped my face in his hands. "It's you I'm worried about now. Fuck that psycho Richardson, if he shows his ugly face around here I'll kick it in. But if my father finds out I'm in Asheville, he'll find out we're together, and he'll go after you to get to me."

A chill went through me. "Shit. Maybe this would be a good time for you to start teaching me some of those Karate moves."

"Good idea. Not Karate, though. I think we should start with Judo."

He looked so sad, I couldn't stand it. I ran my fingers over his cheek. "I'll be okay. We both will. We just have to be careful, that's all."

He tried to smile, but I could tell it was forced. I slid my hand up the inside of his thigh, squeezing and caressing until he smiled for real.

"Let's go upstairs now." I nuzzled his neck.

He chuckled. "You just want to get in my pants, you horn-dog."

"Better believe it." I dipped my tongue into the hollow of his throat. "But mostly I want to forget all this shit for a little while. Escaped serial killers and jackass fathers and the whole damn business."

"Me too." He lifted my face to his and kissed me, then stood up and held his hand out. "Come on."

I took his hand. We went up to our apartment and made love until morning turned the sky gray.

Chapter Sixteen

I had to pester Eric for two more days before he finally called the cops. He made me suffer for it, too. He said if we were going to do this, we might as well get something useful out of it. So we ended up running seven miles across town to The Fresh Market to use their pay phone.

It was one of those perfect days in late October. The sky was that deep, rich shade of blue that seems reserved for October afternoons. The rounded slopes of the mountains rose just beyond the city, the red and yellow and orange of the autumn trees bright in the clear air. Leaves crunched underfoot as we ran, and the miles of rolling hills went by at an easy pace.

By the time we got to The Fresh Market, I was getting pretty tired. It was a perfect day for running, and Eric hadn't pushed me all that hard, but it was the first time I'd gone more than five miles and I was feeling the burn. I leaned against the wall of the building to rest while Eric dialed the police and told his story to the detective they eventually put on the line.

"Okay," he said as he hung up. "Done. Happy?"

"Yeah." I put my arms around him from behind and kissed his neck. "Come on, don't you feel better?"

He leaned back against me. "Well…yeah, I guess I do. Still makes me nervous, though." He twisted his head around to look at me. "We'll do some more training this afternoon."

"Does that mean I'll be falling on the floor for another couple of hours?"

"'Fraid so."

I groaned. Eric had started teaching me Judo the day before, or at least that's what he claimed. So far all that had happened was me hitting the ground, first by myself and then with him throwing me. He said I had to learn to fall without getting hurt before I could do anything else.

I never thought falling down could be so complicated, but there was way more to it than I would've imagined. You have to turn your body just the right way and sort of slap the ground with your open hands. It's not exactly instinctive, so the upshot is that you have to get thrown a lot before falling the right way gets to be automatic. Eric had managed to find some old gym mats at the flea market, so the floor was well-padded. But it still hurt.

"I'm all bruised up from yesterday," I complained.

He turned in my arms and kissed me. "Sorry, baby. You did great, though. You're a natural. We can probably start on some basic moves tomorrow."

"Sounds good. Come on, let's go get some groceries while we're here." I pulled out of his arms and started toward the door.

He stared at me accusingly. "You just don't want to run all the way back."

"Damn straight."

He laughed. We linked hands and headed into the store.

* * *

Over the next few weeks, Eric pushed me hard. Judo training every day, plus a six-mile run every other day. It was pure torture at first, but I improved fast, and that made it easier to keep going. I didn't whine about the pace too much, mostly because I felt Eric's urgency.

He was jumpy as hell for the first week or so after he made that call. He was convinced that someone would somehow find out it was him who had called, and they'd tell his father where he was. The extreme unlikeliness of that happening didn't matter; he was scared. So he did what he could to protect me, which meant teaching me to protect myself.

Personally, I was still afraid of Adam Richardson coming after Eric. He hadn't been found yet, and the police had no leads at all other than what Eric had told them. They'd given a statement on the local news that he might have a cabin in the mountains somewhere, and that if anyone saw anything suspicious to call 911 right away. But almost a month after Eric's call, there wasn't a trace of him and not a peep from Eric's father, and we both started to relax a little.

Relaxed or not, Eric didn't let up on my training. He even wondered if I ought to learn to use a gun. That idea did not engage my enthusiasm at all.

"I don't think so," I said when he brought it up one morning during Judo lessons. "Guns spook me, man."

"That's just 'cause you're not used to them. If you do it enough, you get comfortable with it, just like anything else."

He beckoned me over. I came at him and he flipped me onto my back. He grinned down at me.

"Like that, see? That was a perfect fall, and you didn't even think about it. You couldn't have done that a month ago, but you've been practicing, and now it's second nature."

"I see your point." He helped me to my feet again. "But how the hell do you know so much about guns?"

"Sarah and I used to spend lots of weekends with our mom's parents. I don't think Grandpa trusted Dad much, so he pretty much insisted on us staying with him and Grandma a lot."

"Smart guy."

"No kidding. Anyhow, Grandpa taught Sarah and me how to shoot. Rifles, shotguns, pistols, you name it. I learned to handle a gun before I learned to read, and I kept in practice even after Grandpa died. Dad never knew, or he wouldn't have let us keep going over there. I think the only reason he let us in the first place is 'cause that meant he didn't have to fool with us for a couple of days." He dropped into a fighting stance. "Again."

That meant he wanted me to try to attack him again. That was just fine with me, since I was plenty happy to let the subject of guns drop. I centered myself, keeping my weight balanced like he'd taught me, and tried to think of the best way to take him down. So far I hadn't had any luck at all. He was too damn good, and I was a rank amateur. I could hardly expect anything else, but it was frustrating as hell. Then I had an idea. Maybe I could use his expertise against him. That's what Judo's all about, after all: using your opponent's strengths to defeat him.

I made like I was going to go for his head, and he frowned very slightly, like that would be totally the wrong move to make in a real fight. But he changed his stance to defend against what he thought I was going to do, and I made my move. I grabbed both his arms, dropped, and swept my leg around, knocking him off his feet. He went down. I straddled him and pinned his wrists above his head before he could move.

For a split second, panic flashed through his eyes. But it was gone before I even had time to feel horrified with myself, and he smiled proudly at me.

"Damn, Ben, that was great! You got me! Your pinning technique sucks, but I'll let it slide this time."

I narrowed my eyes at him. "You didn't just let me throw you so I'd feel better?"

"No. That wouldn't be doing you any favors."

"No, I guess not." I stared down at him, trying to make sure he wasn't going to go panicky on me. It had been a while since he'd had a panic attack, but this was the first time I'd actually pinned him. I'd done it totally wrong, but he was still more or less immobilized. "You okay?"

"I'm fine."

I started to get up, then stopped. His hips were trapped between my thighs, and his eyes burned with a sudden desire. I bent down and pressed my lips to his.

His mouth opened in a deep, hungry kiss that set every nerve in my body blazing. When I let go of his wrists, he wound his fingers into my hair and pulled me down on top of him.

We were only wearing loose shorts, so it didn't take us but a few seconds to get each other undressed. Eric pulled me back into his arms as soon as the shorts were out of the way. His fingers traced down my back, and I shivered. We'd been together a few months now, but his hands on my bare skin still melted me just like it had the first time he touched me.

"Ben," he whispered against my lips, "want you inside me, baby. Please."

I pushed up on my elbows so I could look into his eyes. There was no panic in them, no fear. Only love, and desire, and an absolute trust that shook me to the core. He was really ready this time. And I knew that for him, this meant more than just another way to have sex. He was placing everything he was in my hands. It was a gift, and I wanted to treat it that way. I caressed his cheek and gently kissed his sweet lips.

"Yes," I told him. "I love you."

He smiled. "Love you too." He bit my bottom lip, then stretched his arm out to grope under the bed for the lube we'd dropped the night before and never bothered to retrieve. The memory made me smile. My ass was still sore from the pounding he'd given me.

"Got it!" He pulled his arm back and held up the lube. We stared solemnly at each other.

"Promise you'll tell me if I hurt you, or if you want to stop."

He dropped the lube, reached up and cupped my face in his hands. "You won't hurt me. I trust you." He pulled me down and kissed me. "I've waited so long for this, Ben. I need you in me so fucking bad."

I nuzzled his cheek, then kissed my way down his neck and licked at the scar on his collarbone. He moaned and opened his legs for me when I slipped a hand down to stroke his cock.

"Relax," I whispered. "We're going slow on this one."

I ran my fingers down his thigh and he whimpered. "I don't know if I can."

"You can." I kissed the pulse jumping in his throat. "Let's not rush this." I kissed the angle of his jaw, his chin, the perfect bow of his upper lip. "I want to feel every single second."

I bent and sucked one pink nipple into my mouth. He gasped and arched against me. My hand was still wrapped around his cock, sliding slowly up and down its length with just the slightest amount of pressure. I'd learned pretty quick that he made the most gorgeous noises when I did that, so of course I did it all the time.

I let go of his erection, cradled his head in my hand, and kissed him hard and deep before he could react to my hand not being where he wanted it anymore. He was still making those breathless little sounds I loved so much and I let one of my legs slip between his. He sighed into my mouth and rubbed himself against my thigh.

His hands explored me as if he didn't already have every inch of my body memorized. I could feel his heart thudding under my palm as I ran my hand over his chest. He groaned and sucked hard on my tongue when my fingers reached his balls.

"God, Ben. Please, please…" He pushed against my hand.

"Patience, babe." I smiled at him.

"Don't wanna be patient." He took my hand and pushed it downward until my fingers brushed over his opening. His eyes rolled back and he bit his lip. "Yeah, like that. Please, Ben."

I stared down at his flushed face and kiss-swollen lips. His breathing was ragged, his blue eyes dark with arousal. He was so beautiful like this. I reached across his body and grabbed the lube off the floor. He watched, eyes on fire while I squeezed a generous amount onto my fingers.

I rubbed some of the slippery gel on him, pushing lightly against the tight little pucker. He made a sharp little needy sound, and bucked his hips up again. Watching his face, I pushed harder, and my finger slipped inside him.

His mouth fell open and his eyes fluttered closed. His fingers dug hard into my shoulders. "God yes," he whispered. "More."

I worked another finger through the loosening ring of muscle. He shuddered and pulled me into a fierce, bruising kiss. I responded with an urgency equal to his. My cock was achingly hard against his hip, and I didn't think I could wait much longer. Neither could he, evidently. He writhed and moaned while I stretched him as gently as I could.

"Now, baby, now," he gasped, as if he could hear my thoughts. "Fuck me, right now, please!"

Nearly as frantic as Eric, I snatched up the lube again, got another handful, and coated myself with it. He spread his thighs wide. I knelt between them, lifted his legs, and positioned the head of my cock at his entrance. Our eyes locked.

"It's okay," he said, very quietly. "Do it. I love you."

He kept his eyes open and fixed on mine as I pushed slowly past the tight opening and into the satin heat of his body. God, it felt so damn good. I pulled back, then pushed in again, watching his face the whole time. His eyes hazed with pleasure and his pale skin was covered in a sheen of sweat, glowing in the morning sun. I leaned down to kiss him and he wrapped both legs around my waist.

We moved together in a slow rhythm, lips and tongues tangled together, skin sliding against sweat-slick skin. The universe shrank down to heat and friction and the smell of sex. Nothing existed anymore but the two of us, our bodies locked together.

When I felt him tensing underneath me, I knew he was on the edge. I pushed up on my hands so I could look into his eyes. Watching his face when he came was like watching a living work of art. It fascinated me, every time.

"God, Eric, you're so fucking beautiful."

He stared into my eyes, reached a hand up and stroked my cheek. "Harder, baby, fuck me harder," he moaned. "Come inside me."

At that point, I couldn't have done anything else. I sat up on my knees, holding his thighs in my hands, and fucked him in long, deep strokes. The way he gasped and trembled told me I was hitting the sweet spot every time. He grasped his cock and pumped it hard.

His eyes were locked onto mine when he came. The sight of him caught up in the rush of release and the feel of him tightening in waves around me was too much. The pressure in me burst through my skin and I spilled myself deep inside him.

For a few seconds, we were held in a timeless, perfect bubble. Then the waves of intense pleasure ebbed away and all the strength ran out of my limbs. Eric folded me into his arms and we lay side by side, holding and kissing each other while our heartbeats slowed to normal.

He smiled at me and stroked my sweaty hair out of my face. "Love you, Ben."

I grinned at him. "Love you too, tiger."

"Know what?"

"What?"

"We're gonna have to take turns being the bottom."

I laughed. "Was it that good?"

He gave me an evil grin. "Oh, yeah. Hell, I always loved taking it before…well, before. I was afraid I'd never be able to again, to tell you the truth." He ran gentle fingers over my lips. "Don't think I could with anyone else. Not that I want to."

I pulled him closer and kissed him. "Good. Because I want you all to myself."

He laughed and snuggled close with his head tucked under my chin and his arms firmly around me. We lay in a tired, sticky, satisfied heap for a long time. I'll always remember that. It was perfect, because we were in love and together, and nothing could touch us. It was the sort of contentment that only comes when you have no idea what's going to happen to you. And Eric and I had no idea at all.

Chapter Seventeen

I think we both would've been happy to lie there all day. But it was Friday, we both had to play that night, and Eric was bound and determined that we were going to get a run in first. So we got dressed again and headed out into the November chill.

"So where to?" I asked as we walked out into the thin winter sunshine.

"What about heading up toward the Grove Park Inn?"

"Cool."

It was an easy three and a half mile run to the little public park just down the hill from the Grove Park Inn, and we ran that route a lot, taking the back roads to avoid the traffic. We both loved running through the old neighborhoods, with their cozy houses and narrow, tree-lined streets. Sometimes we'd see a little cottage with a For Sale sign out front, and we'd daydream about buying that house and living out our old age there together. It was a nice dream, even though we both knew we'd probably never have the money for it.

When we reached the park, we decided to take a turn through the trails inside rather than heading straight home. We were right in the middle of the park when Eric suddenly cried out and stumbled. We both stopped and I turned to him in concern.

"What is it?"

"Don't know. Something bit me, I think. Fuck, it hurts."

He put his hand to the back of his neck and we both stared at the tiny dart he pulled out of his skin. For a minute we just stood there, stunned. Then he looked up, staring all around us with wide eyes.

"What?" I said. "What is it?"

He grabbed my arms hard. "Ben, listen to me. Run to the nearest house and tell them to call the cops."

"What? Why?"

He blinked and shook his head. His face was suddenly pasty, his lips bluish. I frowned.

"He's here, Ben, he's come to get us."

"What the fuck are you talking about?"

He pushed weakly on my chest. "Go, go get help."

"Eric..."

"Don't argue," he said, gasping for breath. "Just go."

His knees buckled. I caught him and sat down hard on the ground, cradling him against my chest. "I'm not leaving you! Fuck, what's wrong?"

His words were slurred and clumsy now. "Listen...to me... It's...a drug...acts fast...lasts... a few hours...usually... I'll be fine...when it wears...wears off... He's...he's coming...for us... Fucking go!" His eyes rolled back and he went limp in my arms.

"Eric?" My voice sounded panicky. Everything felt distant and unreal. I stroked Eric's face. His skin was cool and clammy, his breathing so shallow I could barely see it. My hands shook and my heart raced. I'd never been so terrified in my life. "God, Eric, wake up, please wake up!"

"Don't bother," said a female voice. "He'll be out for at least a couple of hours, probably longer."

I looked up. A woman was standing in front of us, looking down at me with a chilly smile. She was tall and slim, with long dark hair slicked back into a high ponytail and skin the color of caramel. A real beauty, but her eyes were hard and cold as granite. I glared at her.

"What the fuck did you do to him?"

"It's a combination of two short acting drugs; it has no permanent harmful effects. If he wakes up, that is. I think he will."

"Look, you psycho, I don't know what the hell this is all about, but I'm taking him to the hospital, and you're not stopping me."

"Can't let you do that, Ben."

I ignored her. I managed to drape Eric's limp body over my shoulder and staggered to my feet through sheer willpower and adrenaline. She stepped in front of me, with that sinister smile still in place.

"Get the fuck out of my way." My voice shook with the fear I couldn't hide.

"Sorry, Ben, but you and Eric are coming with us."

I shook my head, turned around and started the other way. I didn't want to know what she meant by 'us,' I just wanted to get Eric away from there. Then a very large, very heavy hand grabbed my shoulder and I was forced to stop. Turning around, I looked way up into a face that I'd hoped I'd never see again. Adam Richardson smiled down at me.

"Hi, Ben," he said.

Cold fear spiked through me. It was all I could do to stay on my feet. Something sharp stabbed my upper arm. I turned my head and saw the woman standing beside me. She smiled and held up a small syringe.

"Nighty-night," she said.

My vision was already going blurry, and I felt numb and boneless. Adam Richardson reached out and plucked Eric from my arms just before I collapsed onto the ground. My head hit so hard I saw stars. A gray haze clouded my vision. I couldn't talk, and none of my muscles wanted to work. I remember a car driving up the winding road that runs through the middle of the park, and the sensation of being lifted. Then everything went black.

* * *

Reality returned in bits and pieces. Sound came back first, in the form of low voices somewhere nearby. I couldn't make out what they were saying. My mouth felt dusty and my head throbbed with a pain so intense it felt like the bones of my skull were coming apart. My eyes refused to open. I tried to move my arms and legs, and that's when I realized I was tied up. Adrenaline shot through me and my eyes flew open.

It took a few blinks before my vision cleared. I was in a small, dimly lit room, with a big floor-to-ceiling cabinet against the wall to my left and a work table to my right. A sturdy wooden door stood open in the wall directly in front of me, and the voices came from the room beyond. Another door next to it was shut. I couldn't tell where it led. There was a small window between the closed door and the cabinet, covered by heavy drapes that completely blocked any sight of the outside.

My head was starting to clear. I tried to think, to figure out where I was and what was going on. I was sitting in what felt like a large wooden chair. It felt smooth and cold against my skin. I shouldn't have been able to feel that. Because it make me sick and dizzy to move my head, I looked down carefully and saw that I was naked, legs spread and ankles secured to the chair legs. It felt like they'd used duct tape. My wrists were taped together behind my back. The back of the chair dug painfully into my elbows, where my weight had been on them for God knows how long.

I shifted as much as I could, trying to get some circulation going. The movement made my stomach churn. I leaned back on my aching arms again and closed my eyes. The last thing I remembered was running through the park with Eric. Something had happened, something had hit him in the neck and he'd passed out.

Everything came back to me then in a sickening rush. I sat straight up, ignoring the blinding pain and the nausea, and cried out. Or tried to. My mouth was covered with a strip of tape.

The voices in the other room stopped, and slow footsteps started toward me. A man I'd never seen before came strolling into the room. He was as average a person as I'd ever seen: medium height, stocky but not fat, brown hair going gray at the temples. His eyes were small and steel gray and cold as the North Pole. He gave me a disturbingly cheerful smile.

"So," he said, "you're my boy's whore. I'm Randy Green. I'm his dad, and here to set things right."

Eric's father. I felt like I'd been punched. For a few seconds, all my pain and sickness and fear vanished in an overwhelming flood of hate. I strained at my bonds, trying to get loose and get my hands on the piece of shit standing there grinning at me. The need to rip his liver out and feed it to him was all I could feel at that point.

He laughed. "Slow down, son, you're gonna make yourself sick. Wouldn't do for you to choke on your own vomit, now would it?"

I glared at him and he laughed harder. "Bet you're wondering where that filthy slut son of mine is, huh?"

My stomach dropped. I hadn't let myself think of Eric being in the same situation I was in, because I couldn't stand it. But if his father had him, it couldn't be good. Randy grinned wider, then walked back toward the open door.

"Monica!" he called. "Y'all bring him on out."

He turned back to me, watery little eyes twinkling with amusement. "They're bringing him now. I'll let you boys say good-bye, because I'm just one hell of a nice guy. But keep it short, and no crying. Act like a man, for God's sake."

He stepped up to me and ripped the tape off my mouth. It felt like most of my skin went with it.

I took a deep breath and started to tell him exactly what I thought of him. Then I saw Eric, and forgot about everything else.

Adam Richardson half-dragged him into the room by one arm. The woman from the park walked a few paces behind. She had a pistol trained on Eric's head. He was deathly white, his bottom lip split and bleeding, and a massive bruise was already forming on one side of his face. He looked as bad as I felt. I wanted more than anything to be able to hold him right then.

His eyes lit on me, and I watched the spark of hope in them die. He turned and glared at his father.

"You said you'd let him go. You promised. You fucking promised!" His voice shook with barely contained rage.

"I lied," Randy said. "What the hell'd you expect, boy? Took me a serial killer, a professional assassin, and a shitload of strong drugs to even get you here! You really think I'd tell you what we're doing with your little whore before I'm ready? Hell, I'm not that stupid. Never should've let you keep on with that Kung-Fu shit; made you too damn hard to handle." He gave a long-suffering sigh and shook his head. "Well, that's neither here nor there right now. You boys get your good-byes out of the way so we can get on with business."

Eric went perfectly still, staring at his father. I'd never seen him look like he did then: hard and cold and deadly. If I'd been on the other end of that stare, I'd have run for my life. Randy Green just grinned.

"What are you going to do with us?" Eric's voice was low and dangerous.

"You're mine," Randy said. "I'm gonna get rid of you once and for all. Monica's a damn good assassin, she's gonna do the deed for me. The woods are plenty big enough to hide your body."

I flinched at the bald statement of his intentions. Eric didn't. "What about Ben?"

Randy Green grinned in a way I didn't like one bit. "Richardson there gets your little slut. That's his payment for helping me find you and get you, not to mention letting me use this nice little hideout of his. Saves me a hell of a lot of money, let me tell you." He shook his head. "Sick bastard. But he helped me, so I help him."

Eric's composure cracked at last, and he lunged for his father. Monica holstered the gun, grabbed him by the hair, and twisted one of his arms hard behind his back. She moved so fast it was unbelievable. Eric struggled wildly, his eyes huge and panicked.

"No!" he screamed. "No, you can't do that! You can't! I'll fucking kill you!" He twisted and nearly got free again. Monica brought her knee up hard into his back and he faltered just long enough for her to get a better grip. She grimaced as she struggled to hang on to him.

"Can't we drug him again?" she called over the string of obscenities Eric was still hurling at his father. "I can't hold him forever."

"I told you, I don't want him killed when he's under the influence! It's just plain cowardly to shoot an unconscious man."

"Well, let's get it over with. I signed on for a clean kill, not a wrestling match."

He held up a hand. "Okay, don't get your blood up. You can duct tape him if you want, until time to kill him. I expected the drugs to keep him weak a little longer than this. Guess he needed a bigger dose."

He handed the roll of tape to Adam Richardson, who wound a length of it around Eric's wrists while Monica held him. I watched silently. I felt numb with shock and disbelief. The second Monica relaxed her grip, Eric whirled around and kicked her in the chest. She rolled with the blow and got back to her feet, apparently unhurt. But her eyes blazed. Randy Green laughed.

"Told you not to get too close. Now go on and put him in the car. Seems like he doesn't care enough about his girlfriend here to even say good-bye."

Monica's jaw clenched but she didn't say anything. She grabbed Eric's arm and pulled him toward the closed door. Eric started struggling again.

"Adam," Monica said through gritted teeth, "can you please come help me?"

The big man didn't say anything. He walked over from where he'd been standing silently against the wall, hooked one hand through the arm Monica wasn't already holding, and pulled. Eric struggled even harder, but the killer was too strong for him, and he started sliding backward toward the door.

"No!" he cried. "Dad, no, don't! Don't give Ben to him! Don't, please, I'll do anything, please!"

"Too late, boy," Randy said. "The deal's made. We shook on it."

I shot a furious look at Eric's father. "Leave him alone, you fucker! Let him go!" I started pulling against the duct tape they'd bound me with. The need to get to Eric was overpowering.

Randy sighed. "Shit. This is just about more trouble than it's worth." He gave me a baleful glance, stalked up to the closed door and threw it open. A blast of cold air blew in. Outside, it was nearly full dark. At least I knew which way was out, not that it could help me or Eric any. Eric's father went outside; the assassin and the serial killer followed, dragging Eric behind them.

"Ben!" Eric's scream was cut short by the slamming of the door.

It was probably less than a minute that I sat there, though it felt like forever. I felt weak and sick, and my body shook uncontrollably. The thought of what that sicko was probably going to do to me didn't even register yet. All I could think of was Eric, screaming my name while they dragged him away from me, his eyes wide and horrified. My mind kept repeating the same thing over and over: they're going to kill him, they've taken him away from me and they're going to kill him and I'll never see him again. Compared to that, nothing else mattered at all.

When Richardson came back inside, all I could do was stare blankly at him. He came toward me with a smile that would've sent me screaming if I'd been capable of it right then.

"Alone at last," he said. "I thought they'd never leave."

He strolled over to the big cabinet, opened it, and pulled out two big canvas bags. "I just can't work with an audience." He hefted the bags across the room and slung them onto the work table. He turned and stared right at me. "It ruins the mood."

If he was looking for a reaction, he must've been pretty disappointed. I felt completely disconnected from what was happening to me. He frowned, then turned back to his table. He started pulling things out of the bags. I couldn't see everything, because his considerable bulk was between me and the table, but I saw enough. Needles, knives, clamps, a drill, and lots of things I couldn't even identify. I remembered that I was naked, bound, and helpless, and a bone-deep terror flowed through me.

I shook my head as he started toward me with a knife in one hand and a pair of heavy-duty pliers in the other. "N-no, no don't, please don't," I begged. "L-listen, let me loose, I'll make you feel real good! How about it, huh? Come on, man."

He sank to his knees in front of me and ran the flat of the knife lightly up the inside of my thigh. The point scraped my testicle and I flinched. He raised his eyes to mine and smiled, and my insides turned to water. He had eyes like a shark: flat, dead, empty as a doll's. The contrast between those blank eyes and his bright, joyful smile made me want to scream. I held it back and tried to get myself under control.

"It's no fun that way," he said. "That's nothing but sex. It's boring. You have to be changed before I can fuck you. I am an artist, Ben. I'm going to do things to you that you never imagined. And you're going to scream so beautifully for me."

He kept his eyes locked to mine as he lifted the knife to my chest. He dug the point in and sliced slowly up through one nipple. I did scream then.

Chapter Eighteen

It would be nice to be able to say I was thinking up a plan for escape while he tortured me. But this wasn't the movies. It was real, and I couldn't think. I couldn't do anything but cry and scream and beg him to stop. He used several different instruments on me, I think, but I can't be sure. After a while, all the pain and terror blurred into a sort of waking nightmare, and I wasn't even sure what was real anymore.

When he turned away from me, I had an irrational hope that he was going to leave, just walk out and leave me there, still tied up in a cabin in the middle of nowhere, but alive. No such luck. He went to the window, parted the curtains and peeked out, then let them fall again.

"Thought I heard something," he said, frowning. "Must've been a bear. Black bears are everywhere out here you know."

I just stared at him. He smiled, lifted a metal rod off the work table and swung it at me. It connected with my ribs and I felt my bones break.

Let me tell you right now, there's nothing that hurts quite like having your ribs broken. I wanted to scream, but I didn't have any breath to scream with. I gasped and writhed in the chair, trying to squirm away from the pain. The blood roared in my head and I fought to keep from passing out. Even as dazed as I was, I knew that if I passed out, that was it. Any possible chance of escape would be gone.

He stood over me with his hands on his hips. "I think you're ready now. I know I am. We can get started."

Get started. I wondered what he had in store for me next if the things he'd already done were just a warm-up. The unmistakable bulge in his jeans told me something of what he had planned.

"Don't," I whispered. "Let me go, please. Please."

He frowned at me. "You know better than that. Now be still, I have to cut your legs loose."

He bent and started sawing at the duct tape around my ankles. I squeezed my eyes shut and tried to think. He freed one ankle, then started on the other one. My mind was going ninety miles a second. I barely felt it when the knife slipped and sliced open the bottom of my calf.

He nearly had my other leg free. I was running out of time. Then it hit me, and I knew what to do. Having an actual plan made me feel hopeful for the first time since they'd taken Eric away from me. Maybe I had a chance, no matter how miniscule, to get away. And if I could do that, maybe I could find Eric. I refused to let myself consider the possibility that he was already dead. Without Eric, there was nothing, and I needed something to hold onto. I took a deep breath, centered myself, and waited.

"Okay," he said. "you can get up now. We're going..."

I didn't give him the chance to finish. When he sat back on his heels and lifted his face to look at me, I pulled my leg up and kicked him as hard as I could, using a technique Eric had just taught me the week before. My heel connected with his face. Bone crunched under my foot, and blood gushed from his flattened nose. He screamed and fell backwards, clutching at his face. I didn't wait to see exactly how much damage I'd done. I got to my feet and staggered toward the door.

Just as I was wondering how the hell I was going to open the door with my hands still duct taped behind my back, it swung open and hit the wall with a bang. Eric stood in the open doorway, covered in dirt. The left sleeve of his sweatshirt was saturated with blood. There was so much of it I couldn't even tell where it was coming from.

"Eric! Fuck, I thought... I thought..." I couldn't finish.

He nodded grimly. "Yeah. Me too."

"You're bleeding."

"Got shot. It's not bad though. God, Ben..."

He looked down at my battered and naked body and his eyes darkened with anger and sorrow. Snatching a bloody knife off the work table, he reached behind me and cut my wrists loose. He'd just tossed the knife aside when something grabbed my ankle and pulled. I caught a glimpse of Adam Richardson, on his knees in a puddle of his own blood, holding my ankle in a death grip. Eric caught me as I fell and lowered me to the floor. I lay there trying to breathe. Eric pried the killer's fingers open and pulled him away from me.

"Fucking piece of shit!" Eric shouted. "I should kill you right now!"

Eric punched the bastard right in his smashed nose, then pulled something out of the waistband of his sweatpants, where it had been hidden against the small of his back. It was a pistol. Eric yanked the other man's head back by the hair and shoved the barrel under his chin.

"Just give me a fucking excuse," he said. His voice was dangerously calm, and I felt a thrill of dread. I knew he'd do it. Adam Richardson stared at him and didn't move. Smart of him.

"Ben," Eric said, "can you reach that roll of duct tape?"

He nodded toward the roll, lying on the floor near my head. "Yeah, I got it." I reached out and grabbed it, trying to ignore the pain in my ribs, and handed it to him.

"Thanks." He smiled at his captive in a way that chilled me to the bone. "Don't you fucking move."

He didn't move. He rolled obediently onto his stomach when Eric nudged him, and put his arms behind his back without even being told. Eric set the gun carefully out of reach, then wrapped several feet of tape around the killer's wrists and several more around his ankles. He used up most of the rest to tie his wrists and ankles together.

When he was satisfied that the other man couldn't move, he scrambled over to me.

"God, Ben, what did he do to you?" He tried to help me sit up. I cried out in pain. He sat down on the floor and cradled my head gently in his lap.

"I-I think he broke some ribs," I said. "He hit me...hit me with a metal rod. Fuck!" I gritted my teeth against the pain.

He ran his hands gently along the sides of my ribcage. My whole body hurt, but when his fingers pressed against my left side I nearly went through the roof.

"Yeah, they're broken all right." His eyes were like open wounds. "Ben, do you think you can walk?"

The thought of even getting up, let alone walking, made me cringe. But I nodded. "Yeah, I think so."

He gave me a wan smile. "Liar. You shouldn't even be moved. But we have to get out of here, and you might end up with a punctured lung if I try to carry you."

I took a deep breath, clenched my teeth, and managed to sit up. "Help me up."

He wrapped an arm around my waist, keeping his hand away from the broken ribs, and hauled me to my feet. The pain was huge. I gasped and clung to him as hard as I could. Gray spots swam in front of my eyes.

"Shit, Ben, you're still bleeding." Eric touched a finger to the cut on my chest, the first one that sick bastard had given me. I looked down. The cut was bigger than I'd thought at first, several inches long and deep enough that it still bled pretty freely. The whole front of my body was covered in red from all the bleeding wounds, but the cut through my right nipple seemed to be one of the worst ones. The worst of all, though, was the one on my leg. Blood ran down from the gaping wound, pooling under my foot as I watched. Eric frowned at the rapidly widening puddle.

"That's a bad one," he said. "You need stitches."

"Doesn't hurt anymore." I smiled at him. He didn't smile back.

"We have to get you to the hospital and we have to find you something to wear. You'll get hypothermia if you go out there naked. We may be out in the cold for a while. Here, sit down and rest while I find you some clothes."

There was nowhere besides the damn chair to sit in the whole place. There wasn't even a bed, Eric told me, just a sleeping bag on the floor. I didn't want to be back in that chair, even for a minute. But I couldn't afford to waste any of the little energy I had left. So I reluctantly sat back down in the chair I'd been bound to only a few minutes before. It was slick with my blood.

Eric brushed the tangled hair off of my face, bent and kissed me. "Only a minute, okay? Only a minute."

I nodded. "Hurry."

He raced into the other room. I sat in the blood-covered chair trying not to look at the man who'd come so close to killing me. Thank God his face was turned the other way. I could hear Eric rummaging around in the next room. He came back less than a minute later with a pair of thick sweatpants, some socks, and a huge down jacket that we could've both fit into. He knelt at my feet.

"Don't know what he did with your clothes, I couldn't find them anywhere." He rolled up an extra sock and pressed it lengthwise to the gash in my leg, then wound a strip of duct tape tightly around it. It hurt like hell, and I couldn't help making little pain noises.

"That ought to hold enough pressure to slow down the bleeding some." He raised his eyes to mine, and the sorrow in them nearly made me forget all about how much I was hurting. "I'm so sorry, Ben. This is all my fault."

"Stop that." My voice was strained and breathless. "Not your fault, it's your father's, the fucker."

He didn't answer me. He pulled the socks on my feet, then started tugging the sweatpants up my legs. "They're too big, but there's elastic at the bottom so they shouldn't trip you. I'll tie the drawstring really tight so they won't fall off."

"Okay," I said. He started to pull his sneakers off and I frowned. "Why're you taking your shoes off?"

"Because you need them more than me. I couldn't find your shoes, and none of his would fit you. I go barefoot all the time, my feet are tough enough." He put his Nikes on my feet before I could protest, then helped me stand up again. I leaned on his good shoulder and tried not to pass out.

"Okay, here. Jacket," he said. When I moved my arm to get it into the jacket sleeve, the broken ends of my ribs grated together, and I hissed with the pain. Now I knew why he hadn't brought a shirt too. I thought I might die on the spot if I had to move my arm again.

"Damn. It hurts."

"I know."

I concentrated and got my eyes to focus on his left shoulder. This time I could see the blood pulsing from a ragged hole in his upper arm. "What about...about your arm?"

"It's fine, don't worry." He picked up the gun, switched it to his left hand, and put his right arm around my waist. "Ready?"

His arm obviously was not fine, but there wasn't much I could do about it right then. I nodded. "Let's do it."

* * *

The night was clear and starry, and so cold the air burned my lungs with every breath. We stumbled along the overgrown dirt road leading away from the cabin, feeling our way by the feeble moonlight. By the time we'd gone a hundred yards or so, the cabin was lost in the forest and I was shaking with cold and exhaustion.

"Gotta rest," I gasped. I started to sink to the ground, but Eric wouldn't let me.

"Can't rest yet. We have to get to the road. Come on, baby, you can do this. Just hang on to me."

"I'm tired."

"I know. But he could come back any minute, we have to get as far away as we can. We have to find help."

I frowned at him. "What? Bastard's back there in the cabin."

"Not him. My father. I got away, but he'll know I came back for you. He's coming, Ben. We can't be here when he gets here."

I nodded. We struggled on.

"How'd you get away?" I asked when I had enough breath to talk again.

"Dad drove us a little ways off, I'm not sure how far. He left us there, don't know why. Soon as he was out of sight, she fired. It was really dark, and I knew she didn't have a night scope or anything, 'cause I'd have seen it. So when she fired, I moved enough so that it got me in the arm instead of the heart and hoped she couldn't tell. I fell down and played dead. When she came to check, I kicked the gun out of her hand, then kicked her in the throat. I got the gun and ran. I don't know if I killed her. She wasn't breathing so good."

He stopped for a minute. He was blinking fast. "Thank God for my dad's twisted sense of honor. He made her untape my wrists before he'd let her shoot me."

"Whatever happens to her, you had to do it." I could hear myself wheeze when I spoke but Eric and I both ignored it. "She was gonna kill you."

"I know." He didn't say anything else about it, but I could tell he was hoping she didn't die from what he'd done to her.

We continued on in silence. I kept staring around at the pitch-black forest. The woods had never seemed ominous to me before, but they did now. I imagined all sorts of things lurking under the trees, and I kept hearing the kinds of noises that you only hear when it's dark and you're afraid.

Just when I was sure we'd spend the rest of our lives creeping through the dark, the barely-there dirt track ended and we emerged onto a paved road. I never thought asphalt could be so beautiful.

Eric smiled at me. "Civilization, at last. Kind of. Come on, let's get a little ways on up the road and find a spot to rest."

I nodded. My strength was nearly gone. Every cut and bruise and puncture on my body ached fiercely, bones scraped together in my chest every time I breathed, and my head felt ready to explode. Eric practically dragged me along the side of the road and finally helped me sit down on a tree stump. He knelt in front of me and held my hands between his palms.

"If someone doesn't come along in a little while, we'll go on," he said. "But you have to rest."

I didn't have the energy to answer him. My head drooped and I couldn't pick it up. Eric sat on the stump behind me and let me lean back against him.

We waited. I kept drifting in and out of consciousness. Most of the time I couldn't even tell the difference. Neither Eric or I had brought a cell phone with us for our run, and I wished we had. The fact that it probably wouldn't have worked anyhow way out in the middle of the national forest wasn't much comfort.

Eventually Eric stirred behind me and sighed. "We should go on now."

The thought of moving again made me feel sick. "I guess."

Eric stroked my hair and kissed my cheek. "I wouldn't make you move if I didn't have to. We're in more danger every minute we sit here."

"I know. Okay."

Eric stood and started to help me up. We both heard the sound of an engine at the same time. Eric grinned at me.

"Stay here, and I'll flag down the car."

I grabbed weakly at his wrist. "What if it's your dad?"

"It's not. He had a rental, all tuned up and quiet as anything. This one's way too noisy to be his car."

He lifted his shirt, stuck the pistol into the waistband of his sweats, and put the shirt back down over it. We didn't have to wait long after that. Headlights shone through the trees, and a battered red Honda appeared around the curve of road to our right.

Eric walked out into the road and starting waving his arms. The car braked just in time to keep from flattening him. The driver's side window cranked down and a dreadlocked head appeared. I could see probably two or three other people in the car.

"Hey, what's the deal?" the young man called out. "Shouldn't run out in the road like that, man, I almost hit you."

Eric walked around to the window. "I know, sorry. But my friend there needs to get to the hospital. We don't have a cell phone with us, or I'd call an ambulance."

"Cells don't work out here anyhow. No towers."

"Can you drive us?"

The guy stared at me, then at Eric and his still-bleeding arm. "Yeah, sure, get in. Nearest hospital's in Brevard. That's where we're headed."

"Thanks, man, for real." Eric turned back toward me. "Ben, come on, we've…"

He stopped suddenly and his face went rigid. There was a moment of perfect stillness, then everything happened at once. Eric whipped the pistol out, the boy in the car gasped and ducked out of sight, and something grabbed me from behind. A beefy arm clamped over my throat, and something cold and metallic dug painfully into my ear.

"Let him go." Eric's voice was calm and his hands steady, but his eyes had that hard, blank look he got when his defenses were up.

"I don't think so." The voice in my ear was Randy Green's. Suddenly I didn't feel tired at all anymore. My mind raced and the pain when he dragged me to my feet felt dull and far away.

"Let him go," Eric repeated.

His father laughed. "Put that thing away, boy, before you hurt yourself. I'm gonna make a deal with you. You come with me, I'll let your bitch here go. That Richardson boy turned out to be a real pussy, didn't he? Laying there blubbering like a baby when I got there. I left him how I found him. I figure he had his chance, and he blew it."

Eric nodded thoughtfully. "So, if I come with you, you'll let Ben go?"

"Yep."

"But you're still gonna kill me."

"Well, we can discuss that. Maybe it doesn't have to work out that way."

Eric was silent. I could tell he was actually considering it.

"No," I said. "Don't, he'll kill both of us, you know he will!"

The arm tightened around my neck and I struggled to breath. "You stay out of this," he said in my ear. "You ought to be glad I'm letting you live, you goddamn pansy."

Eric looked straight into my eyes. "He thinks you're a girl, Ben. You remember what I told you about girls?"

He wasn't making any sense. We never talked about girls, for obvious reasons. Then an idea dawned on me. He'd been teaching me some non-Judo self-defense moves lately, and one of those was something he said they taught women all the time in self-defense courses. I thought I knew what he had planned. Hopefully I was right. I stared hard at him and nodded very slightly. He echoed the movement.

"Stop talking shit, boy." Randy Green's voice rang with impatience. "I don't have all night. What's it gonna be?"

Eric smiled. "Ben'll tell you."

I lifted my foot and stomped as hard as I could on Randy's toe. Thank God he was wearing tennis shoes and not steel-toed boots. His grip loosened, and I drove my elbow hard into his stomach. He let go of me. I dropped and Eric fired the gun at the same time. There was an ear-splitting boom. Randy Green fell backward onto the ground and lay still.

Eric was at my side before the echoes of the gunshot died. He lifted my shoulders and cradled me against him, resting my cheek against his chest. His heart beat strong and steady in my ear. I felt safe and warm, and nothing hurt anymore. When he spoke, his voice sounded miles away.

"Hang on, baby. We're getting you out of here." He kissed me and I smiled, though I could barely feel his lips against mine.

Other voices spoke, and I could sense several people around me. I felt myself being lifted and tried to look around, but there seemed to be a haze over my vision.

"Eric?" I whispered.

"I'm right here." His face appeared over mine. "I won't leave you, Ben. Not even for a minute." He stroked my cheek, kissed my forehead. "I love you."

Love you too, I tried to say. But nothing came out. Darkness and static swallowed the world and I slipped into unconsciousness.

Chapter Nineteen

Someone was whispering. Two someones. I wanted to open my eyes and see who was there, but my eyelids felt so heavy. So I lay there and listened, trying to make out what the voices were saying.

"You're exhausted." A woman. It took my fogged brain a few seconds to realize it was Janey. "Go on home, just for a little while. I'll stay."

"No." Eric. The sound of his voice made my heart race.

"C'mon, Eric, you know I'll call you if there's any change at all. You need to rest."

"I'm fine. I'm not leaving him."

"You're not fine. You haven't slept, and you've barely eaten. The doctor said you needed to get plenty of rest and good nutrition after you lost all that blood."

Blood. Blood pooling on the floor, blood coating my body, blood soaking Eric's shirt, the thick, vaguely metallic smell of it heavy in the air. The memories surged over me in a nauseating flood. I forced my eyes open.

The room had that generic, clinical look that said 'hospital' clear as anything. To my left, a huge window looked out over the mountains. The sun was setting in a blaze of red and orange. Eric and Janey stood in front of the window, heads together.

"Ben lost a lot more blood than me," Eric said.

"Yeah, and he's been asleep all this time and being fed through an IV," Janey said. "You..." She broke off and her eyes widened. "Ben! Oh my God, Eric, he's awake."

Eric whirled around. His face broke into a huge smile when he saw me. He sat down on the bed beside me and took my hand. "Ben. God, it's good to see you awake! How you feeling?"

"Like shit." My voice sounded hoarse and my throat was killing me.

"Here, have some water." Janey picked up a pitcher off the bedside table and poured some water into a cup. "The nurse said your throat would be sore."

"Thanks." I sipped the cold liquid gratefully when Eric held the straw to my lips.

I watched him as he set the cup down and turned back to me. The whole left side of his face was purple and swollen. His eyes were dull, with black circles underneath. He looked pallid and tired. He kept his left arm close to his chest, and I remembered that he'd been shot in that arm. I squeezed his hand.

"You okay?"

He nodded, still smiling. "Yeah, fine. A little banged up, no big deal."

Janey snorted. "Yeah, right. He had to have a blood transfusion 'cause he lost so much from that gunshot wound.

And he hasn't slept or hardly eaten anything since you've been here."

"Thanks, Janey." He shot a stormy look at her.

I frowned at him. "How long?"

"Two days," Eric said. "You were on the ventilator up until this afternoon, 'cause of your broken ribs."

"Jesus." I lifted a hand to touch his cheek, clenching my teeth against the pain in my ribs. He laid his hand over mine, and I noticed for the first time that he had a white plastic bracelet on his wrist.

He saw me looking. "They released me this morning. Don't worry, Ben, I'm fine. Honest."

I tried to sit up. Pain shot through my ribs and thumped in my skull. I laid back against the pillows and tried to breathe.

"You need some pain medicine?" Janey started for the door before I could answer her. "I'll get the nurse to bring you something."

Eric cocked an eyebrow at her back as she left the room. "She picks on me, but she hasn't been home either, and she wasn't even a patient." He leaned down and kissed my lips, very gently. "I'm sorry, baby. I know you're in a lot of pain."

"I'll be fine." My voice sounded weak and scratchy. "How bad were you hurt, Eric? Really."

He shrugged. "It wasn't that bad. Just a few cuts and bruises, and the one gunshot wound. The bullet didn't hit the bone, so even that wasn't as bad as it could've been. They took me to surgery to clean it out and it's fine now."

"Janey said…something about you having to get…to get blood." I stopped, gasping.

"Don't try to talk so much, baby." Eric kissed my forehead. "You have four broken ribs and a concussion, and you lost a whole lot of blood from those cuts. Some of them were really deep. You need as much rest as you can get."

"Tell me." I held his gaze and wasn't letting it go until he told me what I wanted to know.

He sighed. "Yeah, okay. I lost some blood too. But they only had to transfuse one unit. You got three." He stared out the window. The sunset cast a deep red glow over his face. "You could've died, Ben."

I threaded my fingers through his. "I'm okay, Eric. I'm gonna be okay."

He turned and stared hard into my eyes. "I was so scared that night, Ben. You…you were covered in blood, and you were so still. I couldn't wake you up. It was like…" He stopped. A tear rolled down his cheek. "Losing Jason was hell, and it felt like it was happening all over again."

I didn't know what to say. What must it feel like to lose someone that way, and then to have it nearly happen again? He bent to kiss me when I tugged on his hand.

"I'm sorry, baby," I whispered, and using my thumb, I wiped the tears off his cheeks.

"It's all over now. He's gone, and he can't hurt us anymore." He stared solemnly at me. "Is it wrong that I don't feel sorry for killing him?"

"No. You did what you had to. He was a sick fuck, and he deserved to die."

I stopped to draw a few gasping breaths, and Eric shook his head. "Shut up, Ben, you need to rest."

I smiled through the pain. "Make me."

He did. We were still kissing when the nurse came in. We jumped guiltily apart.

"You sure you need this?" She grinned and brandished a syringe. "That medicine looks like more fun."

I tried to sit up again and grimaced when my ribs shifted against each other. "Oh yeah," I wheezed. "Bring on the drugs."

She injected the pain medicine into my IV line and it hit me in seconds. The world turned fuzzy and strange, and I felt like I was floating.

"Now go on back to sleep," the nurse said. She frowned at Eric. "You can stay, but you really need to rest too."

He smiled at her. "I can sleep in the recliner."

"Good," she said as she started for the door. "Oh yeah, your friend said to tell you she was going to get some coffee and she'll be right back."

"Thanks," Eric said. She smiled and went out, shutting the door behind her.

Eric settled himself into the recliner beside the bed. I watched him through a narcotic haze. He took my hand in his and kissed my cheek.

"Stop fighting it, Ben. Go to sleep. I'll be right here."

"'K." My eyes drifted closed. I hauled them open again. "Eric?"

"Hm?"

"Love you."

"I love you too."

I fell asleep with Eric's hand clutched in mine.

* * *

The next two weeks flew by in a flurry of activity. Physical therapy, drugs, instructions on what to do and what to avoid, a visit from Dr. Spencer. I went home after a week and a half in the hospital with a handful of prescriptions and a long list of things I wasn't supposed to do.

The police came by the hospital to question me the day after I woke up. It wasn't as bad as I'd always imagined. They'd already talked to Eric, of course. He'd told them as best he could what happened, and where to find his father and Adam Richardson. The guys who'd stopped to help us -- college kids on a camping trip, I found out -- were a huge help. Not only did they give the cops detailed instructions on how to get to the dirt road where the cabin was, they backed up Eric's story all the way. The driver, Jonah, had seen Eric's dad grab me, and had heard all of his threats. So had the other guys in the car. They'd all said that Eric hadn't had any choice but to shoot.

Adam Richardson had been found, spent a few days in the hospital, and was safely tucked away in the maximum security prison by the time I got home. The cops found a meth lab in a crude cellar under his cabin. Apparently he'd been financing his little torture and murder habit by manufacturing and selling methamphetamine. He didn't use it, oddly enough. Most meth pushers did. They hadn't gotten a word out of him, though. He probably didn't see any advantage in talking. Dr. Spencer told me he probably wanted to keep his fantasies pure. I told her I could've done without knowing that.

They found Monica the morning after the kidnapping, passed out by the side of the road. Once she recovered, she proved to be very talkative. She told the whole story of how Randy Green had hired her to track Eric down, help Adam Richardson escape, and then kill Eric. She'd hidden in an eighteen-wheeler headed west when the driver had taken a break at a rest stop. When the driver came back from the bathroom, she injected him with a lethal dose of potassium chloride. She'd waited until she saw the police van drive by, then followed them in the truck. Randy had followed in his car. Eric's father had helped kill the guards, then they'd all driven to the cabin in the forest. Evidently Monica was counting on getting a reduced sentence for turning in Randy Green. They *forgot* to tell her he was dead until after she'd spilled the beans. She must've been plenty pissed.

They asked her why Randy had wanted Adam Richardson in particular to help him, but she didn't know. He hadn't told her. Personally, I think he was fascinated by what that psycho had done, and wished he could do that kind of thing himself. I also thought that maybe he'd toyed with the idea of letting him have Eric too. That theory, I kept to myself.

If there was a truly positive thing to come out of the whole mess, it was that Eric's faith in the law and the basic goodness of humanity was on the road to being restored. Or maybe 'restored' is the wrong word, since he never had it in the first place. In any case, he was shocked when the police not only believed him about what had happened that night, they'd also believed him when he told them about his past and the things his father had done to him.

"They saw my record." I'd been home for almost a week, and we were rehashing the whole business for about the thousandth time. "But they didn't buy it. They said my version made more sense. I don't get it."

"I do." I poured two glasses of sangria and handed him one. "The cops back in Mobile knew your dad. It's hard to believe the worst of someone you respect, or to speak up against someone who can get your ass fired. The guys up here don't have that history with him, so they can see things a lot more clearly."

He frowned at me. "Should you be drinking wine with the pain pills?"

"Nope."

"Just wanted to be clear, you know."

I grinned. "I haven't had any of the prescription stuff since this morning. Took some Ibuprofen a little while ago, but that shouldn't be a problem. I'm fine, stop worrying."

He had the good grace to look sheepish. "Sorry. I just want to take care of you, that's all."

"I know." I set my wine down and sat down on his lap. "It's sweet."

He smiled in a way that caused all kinds of havoc inside me. "So...doc says how long before you could do anything strenuous?"

I knew what he meant. Parts of me sat up and begged at the thought. "No vigorous activity for eight weeks. Stupid doctor."

He kissed my throat. "Define 'vigorous.'"

"Mm. Um... I guess, you know, moving around a lot."

"What if you don't move?"

"That should be...okay...shit..."

His hand between my legs made it impossible to think of anything but the need burning inside me. I pulled his face up and kissed him hard.

"Bed."

"Yeah."

Even the sternest doctor couldn't have accused us of being too vigorous. Eric wouldn't let me do a damn thing except lie there. Not that I could have anyway. Between the ribs and all the cuts that were still healing, even regular sex would've been horribly painful. Our usual romp probably would've put us both right back in the hospital. Eric was incredibly gentle with me. It never failed to amaze me that the same guy who regularly left bite marks and bruises all over me could be so tender when he wanted to be.

Afterwards, I lay thinking while Eric slept. How he managed to sleep at all after all that had happened, I had no idea. I'd been having constant nightmares, reliving the torture. Sometimes, in my dreams, that sicko would finish what he'd started. He'd rape me, then cut my heart out, and I'd die with Eric's name on my lips. I'd woken up in a cold sweat every night, shaking all over. Eric had finally ordered me to ask Dr. Spencer for something to help me sleep. The pills helped a lot. If I'd even dreamed since I'd started taking them, I couldn't remember it.

Still, with all I'd been through, Eric had endured so much more. Maybe, I thought, you eventually got to a point where your mind couldn't absorb anything else, and you got hardened to it all. I figured that's what had happened to Eric. It made me happy to think that finally, after a lifetime of abuse and unhappiness, he could put it all behind him and lead a nice, quiet, normal life. A life we could share.

A cottony drowsiness crept over me as the sleeping pill took effect. I snuggled deeper into Eric's arms. It felt so good to have his warm naked body pressed against my back, his lips brushing my neck. I closed my eyes and let the soft sound of his breathing lull me to sleep.

Chapter Twenty

My parents and my brother Brian came to town for Christmas. The first thing Mom did, after she got done hugging me and crying, was yell at me for waiting until I'd been out of the hospital for three days before calling her and Dad. She'd already yelled at me over the phone plenty, but she couldn't resist scolding me in person. I didn't really mind, though. It was just her way of dealing with what had happened to me.

Eric was nervous as hell about meeting them. He was sure they'd blame him for everything. I tried to tell him they wouldn't, but I don't think he believed me until he actually met them. The expression on his face when Mom, Dad, and Brian all hugged him and welcomed him to the family was one I'll remember for the rest of my life.

They spent a week in Asheville. By the time they left, Eric had a whole new family. A real one this time, the kind he'd needed for so long. The kind that would love him like he deserved to be loved. I think they were nearly as happy about it as he was.

Just after New Year's, we got a letter from my dad, addressed to both of us. "All right, Dad!" I said when Eric handed it to me, still sealed. "I knew you could find it."

Eric frowned at me. "What the hell are you talking about? Find what?"

I grabbed his hand and pulled him over to the second-hand love seat we'd bought ourselves for Christmas. "He works at the courthouse in Carmel. He's really good at tracking down public records. I asked him to find something for me."

"What?"

I took both of his hands in mine. "I asked him to find where Jason's buried."

His face went white. For a second I thought he was going to pass out. "Eric? Baby, you okay?"

He nodded. "Yeah. Just...I just...you surprised me, is all." His eyes were dazed.

"Sorry. Guess I shouldn't have sprung it on you like that."

"No, it's okay." He bit his lip. "Where? Where's he buried?"

"Let's see." I let go of his hands and ripped the envelope open. The letter was short and to the point. He'd found it.

"St. Augustine," I read out loud. "A private family plot in a cemetery just outside town."

"That's where he was from. St. Augustine." Eric stared at me with wide, fearful eyes. "I never met his family. What if they don't want me to go there? He wouldn't have died if he'd never met me, I wouldn't blame them if they didn't want me to visit his grave."

"No, it's okay. Dad already called and got permission for us to visit."

"Oh, my God," Eric's voice was breathless. "When can we go?"

"Next week. Listen, my dad says, 'Hope you boys don't mind, but I went ahead and booked you plane tickets. You fly out on the twelfth. You've also got a room at The Bayview Inn for a week. It's a nice little bed and breakfast your mom and I stayed at when we went to St. Augustine last year. Everything's paid for. This is a gift from your mom and me to you two. Hope it helps. Love, Dad.'"

I glanced back up at Eric. He looked confused.

"I don't understand. Why's he doing this? Your parents barely know me. And I'm the reason for everything you've been through. Why are they helping me?"

"Because that's what families do. They help each other. And they know that nothing that happened was your fault."

"But Ben..."

"Eric, listen. I love you, my parents love you, my brother loves you in a totally non-gay way." Eric laughed and I grinned at him. "So now you're part of the family, whether you like it or not."

He smiled. "I like it."

* * *

A week later, we'd traded the biting cold of the mountain winter for balmy Florida heat. St. Augustine was a gorgeous town. Every corner was crammed full of history, and Eric had to see it all. He shook me awake early each morning and dragged me off to explore. It was exhausting, but we had a blast. Poking around all the old houses, forts, and churches with him was so much fun that I could almost forget the reason we'd come there.

He was obviously putting it off, and I didn't say anything. It was going to be hard enough without me pushing him to go before he was ready. We'd talked to Dr. Spencer before we went, so we both knew that it was only a good idea if he didn't feel pressured to do it.

Two days before we had to fly back home, I woke up late to find the other side of the bed empty. After a split second of panic, I heard the soft sound of singing from the balcony. I pulled on a pair of shorts and wandered outside to join Eric at the little wrought iron table.

"Hey." I plopped down into a chair.

He took my hand and kissed it. "Hey, babe. Coffee?"

"Definitely." I helped myself to a cup from the tray on the table. There were biscuits too, still hot, and strawberry jam. "How the hell did you get all this out here without waking me up?"

"Come on, Ben, you could sleep through the end of the fucking world."

"Maybe, but I usually notice coffee." I leaned over and nuzzled his cheek.

He turned his head and kissed me. "Guess I've been wearing you out, huh?"

"You always wear me out."

"I meant with all the exploring." He gave me a filthy smile. "You have a one-track mind."

"You love it." I kissed him again. He tasted like coffee and strawberries.

"Sure enough." He got up and sat down on my lap, winding his arms around my neck. "Ben?"

"Yeah?"

He was silent for a long time, but I knew what was coming. I waited, caressing his bare back and running my fingers under the waistband of his shorts.

"I think we should go today," he said finally.

I tightened my arms around him. "You sure?"

"Yeah. I think I'm ready now." He laid a hand on my cheek. "Thanks for being so patient with me."

"Baby, this is all about you. That's why I'm here."

"I love you, Ben."

"I love you too."

He reached down and tweaked my nipple, making me gasp. "Let's go back to bed," he whispered.

"Um. What about..."

"Later." He leaned down and kissed me, light and quick. "Make love to me first." His tongue flitted between my lips. "Please, baby, I need you. Please."

"Since when you do have to beg me for sex? Come on."

I pushed him off my lap and stood up. He pulled me into his arms. We stumbled inside and fell onto the bed already tangled together.

We spent a lazy hour making sweaty, sticky love. He kissed every one of the scars on my chest, stomach, and thighs, just like I always did to his. It had become sort of a tradition with us, a way to neutralize the pain we'd each experienced. Every time his lips touched my scars, it felt like a little of the horror of that night drained away. I felt like he was healing me, one kiss at a time. And when he came and I felt his body trembling against mine, when he gave me that unguarded smile that shone straight from his soul, I thought maybe I could heal him too.

It was after noon when we finally left our room and headed for the cemetery. It wasn't far, according to the directions my dad had emailed me, so we decided to ride the bikes we'd rented from an old Cuban man who lived down the street. It took us about forty-five minutes of leisurely pedaling to get there. Normally it wouldn't have taken that long, but the humidity made the lingering ache in my ribs worse, so we took it extra slow.

We left the bikes outside the gate of the cemetery. The place was tremendous. Huge oaks with Spanish moss trailing from their branches grew here and there between the graves. The air under the trees was cool and green, dappling the headstones with sunlight and shadow. It felt so peaceful.

The private plot owned by Jason's family was in the back corner of the cemetery, set apart by a tall iron fence. I unlocked the gate with the key that had been left for us, and we went inside. Eric clung tightly to my hand as we wandered among the graves. When he sucked in a deep breath and tightened his fingers around mine, I knew he'd found it.

"This is it." His voice shook. "He's here." He turned to look at me. His eyes were huge and pleading, like he was asking my permission.

I kissed his hand. "Go on, baby. It's okay."

He turned to face the headstone. It still looked new, the marble bright and the words sharp. 'Jason Sands, Beloved Son,' it read. A bunch of wildflowers that looked like they'd just been picked lay propped against the stone. Eric sank to his knees, letting go of my hand to brush his fingers over Jason's name carved into the marble.

"I'm so sorry, Jason. I'm sorry this happened to you. But I know that you wouldn't have blamed me. And…and I don't blame myself anymore." He glanced over his shoulder and smiled at me. "Ben helped me see that it wasn't my fault. You'd like him, Jason. He's so good to me. I love him more than anything."

My eyes stung. I moved closer and laid my hands on Eric's shoulders. He leaned against my legs.

"I'll never forget you, Jason. You're the first person I ever knew who truly loved me, the first person I could ever let myself truly love. I did love you, so much. I'll always love you." He rubbed his cheek against my thigh. "If you could talk to me right now, I think you'd say that you're happy I found someone else to love. Because you're the one who taught me what love could be."

He rose to his feet. "This is for you. For everything you gave me." He took a folded piece of paper out of his pocket and tucked it carefully into the grass around Jason's headstone. "Good-bye, Jason."

He turned and walked away without a backward glance. I stood there a little longer, silently thanking Jason for giving Eric the first real love he'd ever known. Touching the headstone, I could've sworn I felt Jason's presence in the air around me. It seemed like he approved. I whispered a thank you to the wind, then turned to follow Eric.

I caught up to him just before he reached the stone archway that would lead us back out into the world. He turned when I called to him. Tears ran down his cheeks, but his smile was bright and peaceful. I pulled him into my arms.

"You okay, babe?"

He nodded against my neck. "I'm fine. In fact, I feel great." He pulled back to look into my eyes. "He's happy for us, Ben. I can feel it."

I palmed his cheek, rubbing my thumb over the corner of his mouth. "Yeah. I felt it too."

"It hurts to say good-bye to him, but it feels good too. I can't really explain it, but it just...it just didn't feel right until now, you know? It's like I had to have that piece of me settled before I could really move on. And now everything's right, and I can put the past behind me and we can get on with our lives. Does that make any sense?"

"Yeah, it does." I pulled him to me and we kissed for a long time.

"Eric?"

"Hm?"

"What was that you left on the grave? That paper?"

"It's the song I wrote for Jason, you know, the one I was playing when you came in and heard me that time?"

I smiled. "Yeah. It seems like so long ago, doesn't it?"

"Another lifetime." He combed his fingers through my hair.

"So you wrote it down, huh?"

"Mm-hm. It's helped me a lot since Jason died, so I decided to write it down and give it to him. He deserves way more than a song, but it's all I can give him now."

I slipped my hands up the back of Eric's shirt. His skin was damp with sweat, smooth and warm against my palms. "Why, aren't you gonna play it anymore?"

He pressed against me, winding his arms around my neck. "I don't need it now."

"You don't?" I brushed my lips against his.

He leaned back a little and cradled my face in his hands. "Singing that used to be the only thing that made me hurt a little less. It used to be the only thing that…" He fumbled for the right words. "It was like taking a drug for pain. It made me feel a little better, for a little while. But the thing that caused the pain in the first place never went away. I used to think it never would."

He trailed off. I waited.

"All those wounds are gone now," he said finally. "I don't need that song anymore, because I have you." His blue eyes burned into mine. "You've healed me, Ben."

My throat closed up and I couldn't speak. He knew what I wanted to say, though. He pulled me to him and pressed his mouth to mine. His kiss was deep and sweet and full of life. I could taste forever in that kiss.

"Come on, babe," he said when we pulled apart. "Let's go to the beach, what about it?"

"Sounds great."

We linked hands and walked through the stone arch into a bright and beautiful future. Our future, together.

෬THE END෬

Ally Blue

Ally is a married mother of two, living in the mountains of North Carolina in the U.S.A. She is a registered nurse by trade and a writer of man-love by inclination. Her husband is a freelance artist, and their children have apparently inherited his artistic tendencies. Thankfully, they have also inherited his singing voice instead of Ally's, which her family will confirm can peel the paint off the walls.

Ally wrote her first story -- a slash fanfic -- in the fall of 2003, after discovering the joys of reading male-on-male sex starring her favorite hotties, who shall remain nameless. She has since branched out into original character fiction, mostly male/male love stories. Her short stories have been published in the e-zines Forbidden Fruit and Ruthie's Club, and she won third place in the Torquere Press 'Melt' short fiction contest in the summer of 2004.

In addition to writing, Ally enjoys traveling, collecting dragons, and trying to scare herself. Her favorite authors include Stephen King, Clive Barker, and Laurell K. Hamilton, and she is a rabid fan of horror movies.

Ally adores music, particularly Radiohead, Placebo, and Beck. She plans to have her iPod surgically implanted as soon as someone invents a way to do that. Hopefully this will mean the end of playing CDs and her children can finally stop telling her to turn the volume down.

TITLES AVAILABLE In Print from Loose Id®

ALPHA
Treva Harte

COURTESAN
Louisa Trent

DANGEROUS CRAVINGS
Evangeline Anderson

DINAH'S DARK DESIRE
Mechele Armstrong

HARD CANDY
Angela Knight, Morgan Hawke and Sheri Gilmore

HEAVEN SENT: HELL & PURGATORY
Jet Mykles

HEAVEN SENT 2
Jet Mykles

HOWL
Jet Mykles, Raine Weaver, and Jeigh Lynn

LEASHED: MORE THAN A BARGAIN
Jet Mykles

INTERSTELLAR SERVICE & DISCIPLINE: VICTORIOUS STAR
Morgan Hawke

ROMANCE AT THE EDGE: In Other Worlds
MaryJanice Davidson, Angela Knight and Camille Anthony

STRENGTH IN NUMBERS
Rachel Bo

THE BITE BEFORE CHRISTMAS
Laura Baumbach, Sedonia Guillone, and Kit Tunstall

THE BROKEN H
J. L. Langley

THE COMPLETENESS OF CELIA FLYNN
Sedonia Guillone

THE PRENDARIAN CHRONICLES
Doreen DeSalvo

THE TIN STAR
J. L. Langley

WHY ME?
Treva Harte

WILD WISHES
Stephanie Burke, Lena Matthews, and Eve Vaughn

*Publisher's Note: The print titles listed above were previously released in
e-book format by Loose Id®.*

Non-Fiction by *ANGELA KNIGHT*
*PASSIONATE INK: A GUIDE TO WRITING
EROTIC ROMANCE*

Printed in the United States
139677LV00001B/150/P